The Fire Children

Abigail van Kraay

Sarah
GRACE
PUBLISHING
Dyslexic Friendly

Copyright © 2020 Abigail van Kraay
24 23 22 21 20   7 6 5 4 3 2 1

First published 2020 by Sarah Grace Publishing,
an imprint of Malcolm Down Publishing Ltd.
www.malcolmdown.co.uk

British Library Cataloguing in Publication Data
A catalogue record for this book is available from the British Library.

ISBN 978-1-912863-62-4

Cover Illustration by Kathryn Scaldwell
Cover design by Esther Kotecha
Art direction by Sarah Grace

Printed in the UK

Contents

DEDICATION

To my boys, Noah Benjamin and Joseph Hosea.

1
WORMS

Something very unusual had happened in the town of Kingswick. All the colour had gone. It had been fading slowly over days and days. It wasn't noticeable at first, but one morning, around Christmastime, young Benji Brook looked out of his bedroom window and smiled to see a robin perched on an evergreen and snow-laden tree. As he leaned closer to the window, his heart grew heavy when he realized that the robin had no red breast. The little bird, dainty and delightful as it was, looked sad as it nipped a dull berry from a leaf whose deep green was disappearing fast. When the colour had been drained from the foliage, the robin with the ashen chest flew away.

It turned out that it wasn't just Kingswick that had lost its colour. Benji learned that the same thing was happening across the entire world. He heard rumours that certain shades remained in remote parts of the Amazon rainforest, but not many people believed it. Colours were becoming just a memory. Benji couldn't even look at a photograph to remind himself; all the pictures had turned black and white too.

Some philosophers claimed that colour remained in the world and it was simply people's perception that had changed. Then there were the scientists who argued that the colour would return once the earth cooled down. Others believed that because of all the toxins in the air, everything had lost its pigment. Most concluded that it was because the world had simply lost its way.

As life went on, the grey world became quite ordinary. Although Benji could vaguely remember some colours, these recollections were decreasing. Pretty soon, some said, there would be nobody left who knew what colours were like.

Later that morning, as grey clouds spun like spiderwebs in a bright sky, Benji Brook swung by his legs from the branch of his favourite tree. His long, luminous hair hung upside down and his arms swung free, making skinny shadows on the grass beneath as he looked across the clearing to the old, black-and-white façade of Kingswick Hall. Benji liked looking at the world from this perspective. He enjoyed the feeling of blood rushing to the top of his head and stretching his body into shapes, like a snake or a tree frog.

"Look!" Benji pointed to a star-shaped hole in one of the many Georgian windows of the old building. "Someone smashed a window!" He was calling to his friend Flo, squatting inside the hollow of the tree. She was digging her muddy fingers into the earth, searching with wild eyes for minibeasts.

As Benji hung like a bat, he squinted at the broken window. "Ozzy Stone," he said, putting his hands on his hips, still upside down. "I bet he did it. I've seen him sneak over that fence with his mates in the dark."

Benji looked over at Flo as she snuck half out of the hollow. The gap was wide enough for her and Star, her greyish Cockapoo. She glanced up at the broken window, let out a big groan and then continued to dig deep into the earth. Star snuffled the ground with his mucky snout, helping to dig holes for her to explore.

"Look what I found!" Flo crawled out onto the grass, her long dusky curls twisting in the sun as she stood and stretched on her tiptoes. She was dangling a long, fat, wiggly worm in front of Benji's nose.

"Tasty!" Benji said, grinning and coiling his body upright like a cobra wrapped around the branch of a tree.

"I've never eaten a worm," Flo said as she released it back into the mud to join a family of other worms writing together in a bed of earth.

"I bet they taste like chicken!" Benji said as he walked barefoot along a thick branch at least seven feet above ground.

"The badgers and the birds will know," Flo said. "Goodbye," she added as the worm wiggled on a bed of mud. "Thank you for helping our earth."

"How the heck do worms help the earth?" Benji asked with a laugh. He performed his usual ninja jump and landed on all fours in front of Flo with a thump. She giggled as he stuck his tongue out towards the bed of worms and wiggled it.

"Worms help to oxygenate the air," she replied. "These are tiger worms, because they are stripy. They used to be dark red. You could see blood under their skin."

They stared at the long fat worms and watched their grey pulsating bodies twist and squirm. They both loved to observe these creatures. Flo would spend hours digging her fingers into the earth. "One day I will be the president of the Earthworm Society, just like the pretty lady we met at the nature reserve on my 10th birthday." Then, stroking the worm, she added, "I miss colour."

"Me too."

The thought of living in black and white forever made them feel as hollow as the tree trunk, so they stood without speaking. It seemed to them that since the colour had gone, the joy had left the people of Kingswick too. It was difficult to say if this had gone before the colour faded or afterwards, but either way, a dark cloud of sadness had covered the town. Most adults they knew had lost their smiles and walked around as if the entire black-and-white world was on their shoulders.

Benji and Flo were determined to keep smiling. Even though they were the opposite of each other in many ways, they went together like black-and-white piano keys. One thing was for sure, neither of them was ordinary. They were in fact quite exceptional. As Grandpa Brook had always said, *be the splash of colour on the black-and-white canvas of this world.* He was the only adult they knew who had still smiled. There had been a glow about him, and a bit of colour left in his cheeks, right up until he breathed his last breath.

"Rainbow!" they hooted as a brilliant white butterfly danced between them. They both loved minibeasts. Rainbow flew close to Benji, hovering in the air then landing on his bare right shoulder.

"Look," Benji cried as the butterfly spread her bright white wings to reveal two black tips and two black spots on each side. The butterfly perched for a second or two, then closed its wings into a crème arrow and shot away in the direction of the river by Witch Wood.

The silence that followed was interrupted by Star barking as he sprung through the long grass towards them. Flo raised herself up on her tiptoes. Her muddied school dress spun around as she called to him. "What is it, Star?"

The dog's floppy ears sprung up and down in the long grass. As he drew nearer, Flo opened her arms as he bounded into her. Her delicate, dirty fingers combed his peppery fur as he yelped and barked and ran around the tree in a circle three times.

Benji watched with his legs apart and his fists on his hips. "He's doing that thing again. He's barking at the tree." Star began to dig at the trunk, in the very same spot Flo had been excavating moments before.

Flo flung herself back down at the bottom of the tree. On her hands and knees, she looked Star in the eyes as he licked her mucky face. He spun around again in three circles, then sat to attention with one paw raised. He was whimpering.

"He's telling us there's something buried right here."

"Dogs don't talk, silly." Benji narrowed his eyebrows as he spoke and kicked the soil with his bare toes. He couldn't read dogs' minds like Flo. But then, like lightning, he dashed into the woods, returning seconds later with two sharp sticks. "Let's get digging then," he said, his eyes rolling.

As they raised their sticks to plunge them into the earth, the sound of a car horn scattered a flock of blackbirds into the white sky. Mr Knightly's voice boomed in the distance. "Flo! Benji! You're going to be late!"

Star yelped and Benji threw his stick down in defeat. "Let's come back after school."

"No!" Flo screwed up her face and continued to dig away at the earth.

"But, we'll be late for school! I reeeeeeally don't want another black card! I've got two already this week and it's only Tuesday!"

Flo dropped her stick, then tightened her fists into balls and groaned.

"We'll come back," Benji said as he hopped on the spot and waved to Flo's dad, who always seemed to be in a ghastly mood. Benji didn't want to be blamed for the gazillionth time.

"You're both filthy!" Mr Knightly croaked when they had run to him. He looked tired, like he hadn't slept for a hundred years. Dark rings circled his eyes. They looked like tunnels. With no light at the end.

The car door slammed shut as Flo, Benji and Star pressed their noses against the window. They both looked longingly at the black silhouette of the oak tree rising into the pearly sky.

They couldn't wait to be back.

2
PIZZA!

Ten minutes before midday, the school bell rang. Flo sat frozen with her little fists clenched, staring at her seventeen silver pencils lined up in a perfect row. She loved pencils. And she loved rows.

"Come on, Flo!" Benji said, hopping out of the doorway. "It's lunchtime! And it's pizza today!"

"It's 11:50," Flo said, looking down into her lap. The bell was ten minutes early and she didn't like her routine being interrupted.

"Yes, Florence," Mrs Electra said, peering over her diamante glasses with her black lips pursed together. "As I've already told you, you have an extra ten minutes in the school hall if you want to join the book fair."

Flo could feel the teacher's ghoulish eyes staring into her. She had studied Mrs Electra's eyes once before. Never again. They made her insides shiver.

To be honest, Flo was not very good at reading other people's thoughts and feelings. In fact, she hated looking into others' eyes, especially Mrs Electra. Strange things happened; it felt like the person was looking right into her, shining a big bright torch into her brain.

There was something uncouth about Mrs Electra, and Flo didn't like that, not one bit.

"I'm not hungry," Flo said.

Mrs Electra gave her a concerned look, but Flo wasn't convinced. It was as if Mrs Electra pretended to care but was really laughing behind her fake face. Flo was convinced she had changed the time of the school bell on purpose just to upset her.

"Well, you can't sit here waiting for the cows to come home. Pack up your things and off you go."

Flo looked down into her lap and clenched her fists tighter. She couldn't understand what the teacher was saying. What did cows have to do with lunchtime? She could never really fathom what Mrs Electra said because the teacher often used phrases like this that made no sense. Flo just pretended to understand most of the time. Like now. Flo placed her silver pencils one by one in her silver case and packed her silver bag. Flo loved silver. It was the only shade in the world of grey that sparkled.

Just then, another teacher, Miss Bennet came to the door. "I'm terribly sorry, Mrs Electra, but there has been a change of plan!"

She opened the door wide as eleven noisy children scuttled into Mrs Electra's classroom. "Uber Club is in here today. We have a leak in room eight."

Uber Club was for people with learning difficulties, including Flo. Flo thought that "learning difficulties" was a very odd phrase because she was in fact the most advanced learner in her class.

Flo reached for her headphones as the children charged into the classroom. The noise made her brain hurt so much it felt like it was going to explode.

Mrs Electra closed her black lips even more and snorted over her computer screen. "Well!" she said. "I'll be lucky if I get these reports done by next Christmas!" Then she rose from her chair until she loomed over Flo like a monster emerging from the deepest, darkest trenches of the ocean.

Like Flo, many of the children in Uber Club found it very hard to read people's facial expressions. To help them, there was a face chart on the wall showing that if a person smiled, this indicated that they were happy. When it came to Mrs Electra, the chart seemed to Flo to be no use at all. No one could tell if Mrs Electra was happy or frustrated. Right now, she was wearing a small smile as she slammed her laptop closed. Flo shuddered at the sound; she had no idea what that expression meant.

Just as Mrs Electra was about to storm out of the classroom, Joanna Woods appeared in her silver wheelchair and stopped the teacher in her tracks. She wheeled in, causing Mrs Electra to step back and stare at her. Her eyes were so wide they looked like they could have popped out of her head.

Joanna wheeled over to Flo and parked beside her. Flo looked up from her lap and smiled.

"Esss?" Joanna asked. She was pointing to the Chess game with her bent arm. Flo nodded and fetched it down from the shelf. It wasn't always easy for most people to understand Joanna's speech, but Flo always knew what she meant.

Flo had two friends: Benji whom she had known since they were babies, and Joanna in Uber Club. Flo and Joanna shared a mutual revulsion for Mrs Electra. They snickered under their breaths as she flapped out of the classroom, slamming the door behind her.

Joanna winced at the noise. Joanna always jumped at loud unexpected sounds and some mean boys, like Ozzy Stone and his cronies, would try to surprise her by dropping and slamming things.

Flo didn't feel the need to pretend to be like everyone else when she was with Benji and Joanna. She enjoyed drawing and reading in Uber Club and she loved playing chess with Joanna. Outside of school, she loved playing in the woods with Benji. Her happy place was outside, in the fresh air and open spaces of the natural world, away from prattling people. She felt free, digging her toes into the earth and collecting worms.

Just then, a boy called Miles Redwood plonked himself down, right next to Flo and Joanna.

"This is my seat," he said, putting his headphones on and pulling out his tablet.

Flo shuddered and clenched her fists. Miles always wanted to sit next to Flo with his smelly tuna sandwiches and his bright screen. Flo had a phobia of phones, tablets and TVs. She was convinced that people were watching her, as if the screens were one-way windows.

At home, Flo loved playing the piano. Although the colour had long since vanished from Kingswick, when she played melodies on her black-and-white keys, splashes of colour would decorate her memory. Sometimes, they came so strongly she would believe the colour had returned to the world. Occasionally, if she lost herself long enough in the music, the faint outline of a man's face with brilliant eyes would flicker like fire and then would fade. Flo would blink and shake her head as though she was dreaming. Once the music stopped, he would disappear, and everything would be black and white again.

Benji's shiny face appeared at the classroom window, interrupting her thoughts.

"Pizza?" he shouted. He squeezed half of his body through the gap and passed Flo a slice of pizza.

"Benjamin Brook! Get back outside!"

Mrs Bennett had spotted him.

Benji wasn't allowed in Uber Club because he always ended up breaking something. He could never sit still. The last time he attended, he knocked Miles' tablet right out of his hands. It soared into the air like a pancake then landed on the table face down. That didn't go down very well at all. When Miles turned his tablet over, it had a crack right across the screen in the shape of a lightning strike. Miles wailed and shrieked, while Flo held her ears and squeezed her eyes closed.

Flo watched as Benji snaked back out and spun off, whizzing through the schoolyard. Flo didn't like Benji bending the rules, but she was so hungry she forgave him and tucked into the slice of pizza. Joanna, meanwhile, giggled and blushed; she liked Benji a lot and loved watching him storm like a tornado around the school.

The two girls stared out of the window as Benji hovered around the apple tree.

"Eere we go a hen!" said Joanna, grinning from ear to ear.

"Will he ever learn?" Flo asked, shaking her head.

Benji wasn't allowed to climb the school apple tree. Sure enough, he couldn't resist the temptation. Mr Crouch howled across the yard when he saw Benji's bright white head pop out of the top like a lightbulb. Joanna giggled. Flo half smiled and rolled her eyes.

"Another black card for you!" Mr Crouch shouted while flailing his long grey arms around and fishing a little book of black cards from his pocket. He drew a black biro from behind his sweaty left ear.

"That's three black cards this week," Flo said. "If he gets a detention, we'll not be able to go out and play!"

Flo's shoulders sagged. She couldn't bear the thought of not exploring their beloved tree with the hollowed trunk at the Old Hall.

3
RAINBOWS

A hoard of children stampeded through the double doors of the school hall, heading towards the bookstalls. As Flo flicked through a thick shiny book on *Climate Change and Atmospheric Science*, Ozzy Stone crept up behind her, leaned over her shoulder and sneered as he saw what she was reading.

Ozzy was short and stocky, but he was also quick-footed. He could be there and gone within a blink, leaving traces of mischief behind him. His skin was dark, his hair a maze of black wiry coils. Despite his wayward behaviour, he was handsome; his jawline was square, his dimples deep, and his big round eyes glinted like obsidian.

Ozzy pulled Flo's headphones from her ears and then let them go. Whack! They snapped back against her head. Flo screamed. Her fists curled and then she began to groan and squeeze her eyes closed. The hall fell silent and everyone turned around and stared at her. Ozzy grinned like the Cheshire cat.

Benji stormed over with a large, hardback book about mythical creatures under his armpit. The free lollypop that came with his new book hung out of his mouth. He stood nose to nose with Ozzy. They thrust their chests towards each other like pigeons. Just as things looked as if they were about to turn nasty, Mr Crouch appeared.

"What's going on?" The teacher's eyes burned into Benji's as he reached for his book of black cards. "Who upset you, Florence?"

"It was Ozzy!" Benji's nostrils flared and his cheeks flushed.

"Wasn't me," Ozzy said.

"What happened, Florence?" Mr Crouch looked at Flo, but she was still groaning with her eyes tight shut.

"Out! Both of you!" As Mr Crouch shouted, his grey forehead filled with furrows. "Any more incidents and you're both in for a black card and a detention!"

Benji scowled at Ozzy. Ozzy grinned as Benji ran off towards the schoolyard. Mr Crouch disappeared down the hallway. Ozzy stared after him, contorting his lips into weird shapes. Then he towered over Flo as she opened her eyes.

"Laters loser, uber scoober." He made an L shape with his hand towards her then he skipped backwards and took off up the hallway back to his mates. Flo stared at the floor, blinking, squeezing her fists into tight balls.

The bell rang and the corridor filled with children as they piled towards the classroom. Benji and Flo poured through the doorway. Ozzy followed closely, staring at their backs with his eyes narrowed.

Flo and Benji sat by the window where the sun was warm. Ozzy sat where he always did, in the corner on his own, where the teacher could keep her eyes on him. Ozzy was often alone. Even though he met his accomplices behind the sports hall for a smoke, he still felt alone. But he told himself he didn't care. When he watched Benji and Flo together, it made his blood boil. He didn't really know why, but that's why he kept winding them up. That, and the fact that it was so easy to get them roiled.

Mrs Electra wrote in large letters, 'SIR ISAAC NEWTON' on the whiteboard. Flo's eyes lit up and she raised her hand.

"Yes, Florence?"

"I know all about Sir Isaac Newton, Miss! He was born on Christmas Day in 1642 and he formulated the laws of motion and universal gravitation. He was an astronomer as well as a mathematician and he ..."

"Thank you for your input, but I am the teacher here, not you!"

Ozzy picked bits of rubber off the end of his pencil and flicked them towards Flo.

Mrs Electra began to speak. "Once, there was a time when colours existed. White light would bend, and rainbows filled the sky."

Several of the children gasped.

As Mrs Electra droned on, Rainbow, the bright white butterfly, fluttered through the window. Ozzy's mouth fell open as he watched the gleaming insect land for a few seconds on the tip of Flo's nose. Then it flew back out the window to join a kaleidoscope of white butterflies flying in perfect circles.

Ozzy couldn't believe his eyes. Out of the grey sky, rainbow prism trails followed the butterfly's wings. Benji and Flo stared at the colourful scene. They were gawping too.

"Stop staring out of the window and get back on task!" Mrs Electra shouted.

Ozzy rubbed his eyes and shook his head. He looked again and the colours vanished. "Must have drunk too much Iron Brew," he muttered.

"But look at all the rainbows!" Benji exclaimed. "Look at the colours!"

All the children leapt out of their seats and huddled at Benji and Flo's window, but all the rainbows vanished before anyone got a chance to see them.

"Get back to your seats immediately!" Mrs Electra roared. "And be quiet, Benjamin Brook!" Her large body looked like it was vibrating and the bouffant on top of her head was wobbling from side to side. "It is not possible for there to be any colours in the sky! Do I have to remind you that this is a colourless world?"

Flo's hand shot up.

"What is it, Florence?"

"Black and white are colours, Mrs Electra. That means you're wrong. We are not living in an entirely colourless world."

"Be quiet, Florence Knightly! I've had quite enough of your cheek! And you, Benjamin Brook. Now, back to your seats everybody, and a black card for you. You ridiculous boy!"

All the children settled back down at their desks and stared at Benji.

"Loser!" said one boy.

"Weirdo!" said another.

Ozzy grinned.

Benji slumped back down and thumped the desk.

Ozzy tried to convince himself that because he had stayed up so late playing games on his console that he must have been hallucinating. But then he couldn't help feeling uneasy when he saw Flo gaze back out of the window and smile as her dark, deep, pretty eyes looked up into the grey sky.

4
THE BOX

At precisely 3:30pm, Benji and Flo dashed out of the school gates, shot through Witch Wood and reached their tree by Kingswick Hall in record time. They retrieved their sticks and dug deep into the earth, disturbing several worms. Flo placed them to one side.

Star howled like a wolf and snuffled the ground as Benji dug deeper. By now, Benji was quite filthy but being caked in mud was when he felt at his best. He scraped the earth with his stick and cut away some thick, strong roots with the silver pocketknife his Grandpa had left him for his 10th birthday. A few inches deeper and his stick snapped in half.

"Whoa!" he cried, his eyes bulging.

"What is it?"

"Something rock solid!"

"Do you think it's a coffin?"

"If it is, we might find something valuable!" Benji giggled. Then he saw a look of terror flash across Flo's face.

"Don't worry. If it was a coffin, it would be six feet underground."

Flo began to loosen her fists.

Benji crouched low and dug away at the earth. "It's wooden," he said as he clawed away the soil and pulled at the tree roots.

"Maybe it's a treasure chest?" Flo said.

Benji shovelled some earth away, revealing a wooden box, like a treasure chest, but smaller. It had an iron handle attached to its dark oak wood.

Flo noticed a strange word engraved into the wood. Her fingers traced the engraving. It was written in a language that neither of them could understand. Above the words were some musical notes.

♪♪♩♬♩,♪♪♩♬♩

"Can you read that?" asked Benji.

"I'll try." Flo began to hum the tune. Benji's big eyes brightened. The sound made shivers tiptoe up and down his spine.

Just then, hundreds of moon-white butterflies swooped overhead and danced in figures of eight above them in a magnolia sky.

As the creatures continued to fly above, Benji took out a grubby tissue from his pocket and wiped the handle of the box as best he could. The oval plate was in the shape of the sun. It had an eagle's head festooned upon it. The ring had a carved snake protruding from the eagle's mouth.

"We need to hack these roots away," Benji said.

Flo took a step back as he cut away at the roots entangling the box.

"It looks like it could have been here for hundreds of years," Flo said.

Benji put his right foot on the box and gripped the handle with both hands. He pulled with all his might, but it would not budge or open.

Just then, Star yelped.

"Benji! Flo! Where are you?" It was Benji's mum shouting in the distance.

Again, Benji pulled with all his strength, but it was securely shut.

Mrs Brook continued to call.

"Coming!" shouted Benji. They kicked earth and sticks over the box to try and cover it as best they could. Then they ran across the lawn towards the stone steps of the old hall where Mrs Brook stood waiting.

"I wonder if there's a key," Benji mused.

"But there's no keyhole."

Benji wiped the mud and sweat from his forehead. "It must open somehow!"

"What on earth have you been doing?" said Mrs Brook as they ran to the car where she was waiting. "You're covered in mud!"

Benji's mum always looked worried these days. Her frown had got deeper and deeper in recent weeks. The more Benji whirled around like an F5 tornado, the gaunter she had come to look.

As they reached the vehicle, they all looked up to see the brooding clouds swirling in the sky. The next moment, there was a downpour of rain.

Muddied and soggy from head to toe, they clambered into the black-and-white car. The setting sun sent shafts of white light through the rain. Liquid beads trickled down the windscreen and for a split second, beams of light danced through the glass, making rainbow patterns on the children's skin.

Then the sky darkened. The car began to steam up as the rain fell heavily and lashed against the windscreen.

The next moment, the car jolted to a halt.

"Sorry!" Benji's mum cried. "I don't know what that was! I nearly hit a cat, or something. Seemed bigger than a cat. Just missed it by an inch."

Both the children saw a four-legged creature run past the car and disappear into the woods.

"A badger, maybe? Poor thing. Hope he's okay."

Benji and Flo squinted through the line of trees. They could now see the black figure standing. It was on two legs, right next to their tree. Star yelped from the back of the car and howled at the granite sky.

"Can we come back to the Old Hall tomorrow, Mum, please? We've found a treasure chest buried in the ground!"

"We'll see," she said, with little hope in the tone of her voice. "Not sure this rain will hold off."

Benji could tell she did not believe them, but he turned to Flo with a wild look in his eyes as the car drove through Kingswick in the lashing rain.

Flo stared back, her fists curled up into tight balls. Benji felt like he might explode with excitement as he wriggled in the back of the car. He wondered what could possibly be inside that wooden box, and although it took a lot to spook him, he did feel the hairs stand on the back of his neck and goose-bumps all over his body as he turned back to the tall dark figure, lurking by their favourite tree.

5

MOON QUEEN

Flo drew a circle with her fist on her steamy bedroom window. The sky was starless and clear as she looked through her makeshift porthole towards Benji's bedroom across the street. His light was still on, so she made their secret whistle. Just when she thought she saw his silhouette, Benji's mum closed the curtains. Flo sighed. She drew a butterfly on the window and lay on her bed.

Flo's bedroom was otherworldly. Hundreds of silver pencils were displayed in rows of jars on a floating shelf. There were brilliant black-and-white sketches and magazine cuttings of the earth and the sun lining her walls, along with pictures of polar bears, penguins, fish, beasts and creatures of every kind. Scores of paper butterflies and birds hung from the ceiling. Many of Flo's sketches were framed in silver with fairy lights above them. Two large bookcases were also crammed full of encyclopaedias and books on minibeasts, ecology and astronomy.

Flo listened to the usual sounds of her mum and dad arguing downstairs. They made her heart heavy, so she grabbed her silver earphones and switched her mind back to her and Benji's mysterious day. As she lay on her bed, worrying that she would stay awake with her mind so busy with worms, badgers, rainbows and butterflies, she fell without any hesitation into a deep sleep.

No sooner had she drifted off, than there was a fluttering at her window. In flew Rainbow. The white butterfly flew towards her and made vibrant rainbow trails above her sleeping head. Then, with a few flaps of her wings, she had left the room and disappeared into the night.

In her dream, Flo found herself shivering. She was crouching in a muddy wet ditch. The moon was full. She looked up at the golden light, staring at its colour in unbelief. The moon shared enough light for her to see the mysterious box that she and Benji had found. It was lying in the ground.

Flo's fingers snaked the musical notes etched into the wood. She tried to hum the tune again as her teeth chattered. Suddenly, she was met by a strong breeze and the great oak shook, its leaves showering Flo. She fell back in the ditch in terror.

"What's happening? Benji, is that you?"

Then she heard a gentle whisper.

"Arise!"

Then a multitude of whispers singing in unison.

"Arise! Arise! Arise!"

The wind now howled. The tree shook and a myriad of tiny lights began to dance all around her, lighting up the night.

Flo blinked.

They were butterflies, hundreds of them all lit up like moonbeams, leaving rainbow trails like the ones she had seen outside her classroom window. They swirled all around her and then disappeared into the hollow of the tree.

Flo shuddered as she heard a loud snapping sound, like a branch breaking.

She swivelled around.

A tall, dark hooded figure was standing by the oak tree, stretching out its white hands. From the folds of the cloak, a thick black snake began to emerge, coiling around the arm protruding from it.

Just as Flo was about to scream, the moonlit butterflies reappeared and grouped together to create the shape of a figure twice the size of the dark and sinister intruder. These airborne lights morphed into a luminous woman. She seemed to be wearing a flowing dress in the same bright yellow colour as the moon. She towered above him, about twelve feet tall, and her enormous iridescent wings filled the sky. Her long golden hair shone like the sun and her eyes shimmered like amber.

"Don't be afraid, Flo!" she said. "The terrors of the night are no match for your King." She smiled so kindly that the air seemed to be alive with peace.

Flo looked straight into her eyes and felt no fear. She had never dared to do this before with a stranger, but with her, she felt she could do this forever.

Just then, the radiant woman sang using the tune from the musical notes etched into the wooden box.

"Arise, Fire Child! Arise! Arise! Arise!"

The woman then spread her wings and flew into the dark night, disappearing into the wide moon in the clear black sky.

"Who are you?" whispered Flo as she looked up.

The air was silent. The wind, the whispers, the howls had gone, and the dark figure with them.

"Arise!" Flo whispered.

She felt a warmth hugging her body, even as the cool of the night touched her brow. She was so calm she thought she could float.

As she lay on the ground and gazed up at the sky, she sang, "Arise! Arise! Arise!"

When Flo woke up, she was tucked up in bed and her mum was dabbing a cool wet flannel on her forehead.

"Mum?"

"It's okay, sweetheart. You were just dreaming. You must've caught a chill today."

"Arise, Mum! Arise! Arise! Arise!"

"What are you talking about?" Her mum frowned. "Calm down and have a sip of water."

"I saw a woman lit up like the moon. I saw gold. The colour gold! And she told me to arise…"

"Shhh now! You'll wake up your sister." Flo's little sister Bea was asleep in her bedroom across the hallway. With her door wide open, Flo could see her face peeping out of her duvet, sleeping like a little angel.

"It was just a dream," Flo's mum insisted.

"It wasn't a dream, Mum. She must be an angel. She was bright, like fire, and the moon was gold and…"

"Florence Knightly, you have an overactive imagination. You can write your stories tomorrow. It's time to sleep."

"Are angels real, Mum?"

Mrs Knightly paused as though she was about to say something, but then the lines above her eyes grew more pronounced, and she shook her head.

"Now is not the time for questions. Go to sleep."

Flo leaned back into her pillow as her mum turned out the light, leaving the door ajar as she left. Flo's dad was already asleep in his bedroom and snoring loudly. Her mum disappeared down the hallway to the spare bedroom and closed her door. They had been sleeping in separate beds for a long time. Mrs Knightly said it was because Mr Knightly snored, but the truth was something had changed since Flo's baby sister had died. She only lived for one hour after she was born, and from the moment her heart stopped, it seemed like her mum and dad were so sad that they had forgotten how to smile. Flo grieved for the way things used to be before the shadows filled their home. Her mind drifted back to when her mum and dad would let her crawl between them in their king-sized bed in the middle of the night. She used to love burrowing into the nook of her dad's armpit and telling him all about how penguins are aquatic flightless birds that spend half their lives swimming and half their lives on land.

Flo jumped out of bed and opened her curtains to see the moon high in the night sky. It was almost the same moon as in her dream, except that it was large and white, not gold. She sighed and then hurried back to her warm bed. As she thought about the Moon Queen, the sadness slipped away.

Flo was happy.

Happy that at least the colour had not been stolen from her dreams.

6

GRANDMA BROOK

Mrs Brook was trying to drive her car when Little Jo looked up with his big, bright eyes and pointed to the clouds. "I can see a pig!" he cried. Little Jo was named after their Grandpa Jo. He looked just like him, although much smaller and cuter.

"I can see a crocodile!" Benji said, launching himself out of his seat and snapping his arms together around his little brother's head. Little Jo squealed.

"Boys!" Mrs Brook cried. "I am trying to drive! Get back in your seat, Benjamin Brook!"

As the car pulled up, Benji leaned back and squinted at the granite cloud above Grandma Brook's cottage. For a moment, he was convinced he could see a dark creature with wings. But then, after he blinked, the cloud became just a cloud again. Benji pressed his forehead against the window as the rain whipped it. There was not a chance that he and Flo would be able to visit the Old Hall. The rain was too heavy.

The boys clambered out of the car holding a warm tray of cookies and headed towards the cottage. The garden was overgrown but teeming with life. Lavender, fresh mint and rosemary scented the air.

Black-and-white roses grew high and wild up the fencing. Cobwebs hung in the corners of the wooden window frames. Dark ivy covered the cottage and the branches of the trees were heavy with fruit.

Early September was the perfect time for picking, so Benji balanced the tray of cookies in one hand and reached for a juicy pear with the other. The tree shook and fat beads of rain saturated Mrs Brook and Little Jo just as several ripe pears fell to the ground.

"Benjamin Brook!" his mum shouted as she wiped the rain from her wet face. "We haven't been here thirty seconds!"

"I was just picking a pear, Mum."

Pear juice was now dripping down Benji's chin as they walked along the winding pathway, the wet brambles catching their ankles.

"Mum! We're here!" Mrs Brook called out as they entered the cottage and Benji finished his pear.

Benji kicked his shoes into a pile of his grandpa's old shoes by the front door. As he walked in, Finn the cat curled his thick grey bushy tail between Benji's legs. Benji picked him up, nuzzling his face into his fur. Then, carrying his tray of cookies as well as holding Finn, he shuffled into Grandma Brook's kitchen and plonked the food on her crowded table.

Grandma Brook's cottage was like a dark cave filled with all sorts of weird and wonderful objects. Grandpa Brook had been a collector and he had travelled all over the world. On almost every wall, corner and surface, Benji could see a picture, a glass ornament or a trinket from a faraway land. All except one corner of the room, where a tall easel and some canvases leaned against the walls. Most were blank, but several had a few unfinished brushstrokes in black and grey. Old crusted-over paint pots and brushes were strewn across the floor. Grandpa Brook had been Benji's hero. He missed him so much that every time he visited the cottage, he felt a great big lump in his throat.

Grandpa Brook had died a year ago. He was a jolly old man who used to tell many tales. During his final days, he became very forgetful, and his tales became more and more fanciful and mindboggling. Benji loved to sit by the fire with his grandpa, play the mandolin and sing seafaring songs. His favourite story was when his grandpa sailed to Patagonia and there was a great storm. He told Benji that he had fought a fierce green dragon with his bare hands and met a Fire King with eyes that burned like amber and gold. All his sailing companions who hadn't see the dragon and the king thought Grandpa was mad, except when he used his special power to calm the sea.

"There's more to life than what meets the eye," Grandpa Brook used to say with a knowing wink.

Then, before he drew his last breath, he had said to Benji, "Never forget little one, colour returns to those who believe."

Then his sparkly eyes - which had never quite lost their blue - slowly closed. Grandpa Brook's smile remained etched upon his lifeless face, and although his kind heart was as still as a stopped clock, his skin was still warm and pink as Benji sobbed into his chest. Mrs Brook said Grandpa had died with a head full of nonsense, but all Benji saw was a glow under his skin. He loved his stories and he believed they were real. When Grandma Brook would say, "He's lost his marbles," Grandpa would wink and say, "My marbles are perfectly fine. They're kept in a jar on the mantelpiece." This always made Benji laugh. He didn't quite understand what he meant, but there was a large glass jar full of marbles on his mantelpiece, among all his many paintings and trinkets. "It's just that warped imagination of his!" Grandma Brook would say. "The truth is, little feller," Grandpa Brook would add, "Who's to say that what is in your imagination is not real? Have you ever thought about that?" He would tap his old head while he whispered.

When Grandpa Brook died, it felt like he took all the colours with him. He was the only adult that Benji could think of who smiled, the only one that did not get upset with the news of doom on the television. In fact, he didn't watch much television. He said life was too exciting to be staring at a screen all day long, and that it was the screens that were sucking our souls out of our bodies and stealing all the colour away.

After he had died, the cobwebs grew and the dust thickened in Brook cottage. Grandma Brook stopped cooking. She nibbled on grey cheese and raisins all day long while watching the giant black-and-white television that she had bought after the funeral.

"Have you seen this?" Grandma Brook said as her old grey whiskers twitched. She spluttered some spittle across the room towards the giant television. Benji grimaced, then his shoulders began to tremble. Little Jo looked fit to burst as they tried very hard to hold their giggles inside.

Grandma Brook pointed her old shrivelled arm towards the screen. "What has the world come to, eh? It's not fit for purpose these days. These blasted politicians, tearing the country apart. They haven't got a clue how to deal with a crisis!"

On she went in her usual monologue of despair.

"It just gets worse," Benji's mum said, adding to the gloom.

Benji and Jo stared at Grandma Brook. She looked even older than the last time they saw her, which was only a few days ago. Her hair was whiter, her voice raspier and her grey eyes seemed to be getting smaller as though they were fading away. The doctors said she had an incurable disease.

Benji stopped snickering and suddenly felt quite glum again. He wished she had the same joy that Grandpa had before he died. He always said it was like a bubble that would never pop. But she didn't seem to believe in anything if you could not see it. Grandpa, on the other hand, used to say he was looking forward to dying. "That's when the adventure begins," he would add.

Grandma Brook sat in an old leather armchair whose creases matched the ones in her old wrinkled face. Her frown was engraved like stone as she stared at the enormous television suspended on the chimneybreast.

Just then, Benji thought he caught sight of something out of the corner of his eye. A dark shadow the shape of a monkey seemed to be hiding behind Grandma Brook's armchair. It crept across the wall towards the window. Benji blinked and rubbed his eyes. When he looked again, it was gone. He glanced at Jo and his grandma to see if they had seen anything, but it all happened so fast he wondered if his mind was playing tricks again.

Benji walked to the burner and built up a small fire. The room filled with a warm glow as the kindling began to crackle. Then he lay on the patchwork rug with his arms folded behind his head, his eyes drifting along the mantelpiece, where the jar of marbles stood amongst some old dried flowers, an old mandolin with broken strings, several peculiar pictures and some glass carvings from faraway places.

Benji sat up, and then clambered onto a little wooden stool to grab the jar of marbles. As he stretched on his tiptoes, a row of small paintings and sketches in silver frames toppled over like dominoes and fell to the ground.

"What are you doing up there?" Grandma asked.

"Sorry, Grandma. I was just fetching the marbles."

Then he started to pick up the objects that had fallen at his feet.

"Did Grandpa draw these pictures?"

"I always said, we needed a bit of wall space to breathe, but he insisted on cramming every bit of space with his clutter." Then Grandma Brook turned up the television to the loudest volume. Poor little Jo held onto his ears.

As Benji placed the small pictures back on the shelf, he noticed there was a caption underneath each painting. The first painting was a picture of a tree and a light coming from the hollow in its trunk. Benji's eyes expanded.

Could this be his tree?

Then his eyes almost popped out of his head when he noticed underneath the painting a small glass plaque. There were three words on it:

Arise! Arise! Arise!

Benji's heart seemed to miss a beat.

He stood back on the stool and looked at the other pictures. Another caption read:

Follow the butterfly

This was accompanied by the picture of a butterfly, a snake and a sword.

"What are you looking at, Benji?" asked his mum as she entered the room with a tray of tea and cookies.

"Grandpa Brook's paintings."

Benji grabbed a handful of cookies. He shoved two in his pocket and stuffed the rest into his mouth. He stared at another picture, this time of a big cactus. He felt as if there were a hundred butterflies fluttering around inside him. All he wanted now was to tell Flo and return to the tree.

He looked out the window and punched the air with his fist.

"Yes!" he cried, as a slither of sun finally escaped through the clouds.

7
BLUE

Benji hopped on the spot and pounded his fist on the black-and-white door of the Knightlys' house. Mrs Knightly answered.

"What is it Benji, is everything ok?"

"Can Flo play out? It's a sunny day."

"Good grief, boy! The way you almost knocked the door down, I thought someone had died!" Then she turned around and shouted, "Flo! Benji's here!"

Flo ran down the staircase with her coat on and she was out of the door before her mum could catch her next breath.

"Come on, Star!"

Flo whistled as Star bounced after her, his curly spaniel ears flopping up and down. He was howling like a wolf at the sky.

"Be back for supper! Before dark!"

Mrs Knightly's voice faded into the distance as Benji, Flo and Star ran down Silver Birch Lane and across the field, towards Witch Wood, taking a shortcut to the old hall.

"I've so much to tell you!" said Benji, panting.

"Me too!" Flo said. "I had a dream. I met the most beautiful lady filled with the light of the moon! She was like an angel, and she sang,

'Arise! Arise! Arise!' The same tune as the notes we had found on the box!" Flo's eyes were wild.

Benji let out a loud squeal and leapt in the air. He spun around in circles like Star.

"Our tree is in one of my Grandpa's paintings!" he cried. "And under the painting it said the same thing, 'Arise! Arise! Arise!'"

Flo gasped. "Do you think it's the same tree?"

"It must be! But there's only one way to find out!"

They climbed the fence at the edge of the field, skipped over the stream, through Witch Wood and came out behind the Old Hall where the vegetable garden grew. Giant pumpkins were set out in rows alongside squash and tall grey maize.

"Not long until Halloween," said Benji with his eyes gleaming.

Flo shuddered.

"Perhaps this is not a great idea after all," said Flo.

"Are you crazy? This is a sign! Tell me about the lady. What was she like?"

"She was made of butterflies and moonlight and she had the loveliest eyes. I didn't feel scared to look at her. I felt like I was floating. She was twice as tall as the dark one, she was a golden colour and…"

"The dark one?"

"There was a tall, dark figure. I think it was the one we saw yesterday. It wore a black coat with a hood up. I couldn't see a face. It had long white arms and a black snake came out from under its sleeves. Then the bright lady came, and it disappeared."

"This is so cool!"

"Scary!" said Flo.

They reached their beloved oak tree. Dappled leaves, twigs and broken branches covered the hole they had dug the day before; it had been a windy night. They scooped them out of the way and pulled the box out of the cavity. Star stood above and barked while they both crouched low at the foot of the tree.

"What do we do?" asked Flo.

"Open it!" said Benji.

Flo's eyes were wide with fright.

Benji took a deep breath and gripped the iron handle. Just as he was about to pull, the metal ring turned black and began to squirm like a snake in his hand. He screamed and recoiled in horror. But then the handle turned back to normal again.

"Did you see that, Flo? The snake was real!"

"I saw it! It's not possible! We'd better go home, this is weird!"

"No! Grandpa Brook wouldn't paint this picture for nothing. There must be something really important in this box."

Flo squeezed her eyes closed. She wasn't as brave as Benji. Benji gripped the handle and just as he pulled with every fibre of his being, Rainbow the butterfly appeared above him. Then the lid flipped open.

The two friends peered into the box. Their jaws dropped as they gazed inside and saw a mandolin, a scroll of paper and a small glass lantern.

Benji picked up the mandolin. It was just like his grandpa's, but the wood shone, and the strings were tight.

Flo grasped the glass lantern and marvelled at the grey stripes painted on the unlit glass.

Benji unfurled the small scroll of paper. There were some musical notes and lyrics above them. "I can play a little, but I can't read the music."

"I'll sing and you play," Flo replied, taking hold of the scroll.

Benji smiled and nodded as Flo read out the notes.

"E, B, G, D, F, A, E…"

Benji began to play. He sounded a little rusty to begin with, but then he caught the tune and his fingers began to flow.

Rainbow and a kaleidoscope of butterflies fluttered around the tree as Flo sang the lyrics to the music written on the paper scroll.

Arise Fire Child
Resolute and wise
Raise your weapons to the skies
Colour will return
To an ashen world
When the Shadow Prince is defied

Arise Fire Child
Arise, arise, arise

Flo sang over and over, and a beautiful sound filled the air. Hundreds of butterflies danced above them, and every black and grey bird of the air came to perch in their tree.

"Blue!" Flo blurted out mid song, as the wick inside the oil lamp burst into a blue flame.

Rainbow fluttered between them, then disappeared inside the hollow of the tree. Flo and Benji followed. They crawled inside with the burning lamp. To their surprise, it didn't seem so very small anymore. As the blue flame lit up the dark of the hollow, they stood up tall and looked around. It smelt damp and woody. Then they saw a set of spiralling steps that lead downwards for what seemed like miles. The small flame grew bigger and flickered blue and purple and yellow gold.

"Follow the butterflies!" Benji shouted, recalling the message from Grandpa's pictures. He grabbed hold of Flo's closed hand. She took a deep breath, hooked Star on his lead and they stepped down into the belly of the earth.

After descending what felt like a thousand steps, they found themselves inside a dark, tall, enchanting cave. They were deep below the earth's surface and surrounded by limestone. As they reached the bottom step, their mouths fell open.

"Stalactites," Flo whispered. Thousands of solid icicles hung like organ pipes from the ceiling of the cave.

"Where are we?" Benji asked as he looked up at the roof of the huge cave, his voice echoing throughout the chamber.

"This place is thousands of years old," Flo said. "These stalactites are made of a sort of liquid acid that's been dripping slowly for thousands of years."

No sooner had she said this than a huge, bright blue butterfly, the size of a man's hand, fluttered between them.

"Wow!" exclaimed Flo, "look!"

"Follow the butterfly!" Benji cried. "Come on! Let's go!"

They followed the insect as it swooped in and out between them and fluttered around corners and bends. The children climbed over rocks and squeezed though clefts as the creature led them deep into the cave and towards a pool. A shaft of light from a crevice in the ceiling of the cave shone on the water and the pool lit up in electric blue.

"Your eyes are blue!" Flo beamed.

"And yours are brown!"

"And look, Star's eyes are golden!" cried Flo. Star yelped as though he too was excited to see colour again.

The pool was deep and so clear that you could see rocks of many colours and the trunks of ancient trees underneath the still and crystal-clear water. As their eyes imbibed all the colours, they both saw something at the bottom of the water. It looked like a sword, glistening in the silt.

"Look at that," Flo continued to whisper. "How do we get it?"

"Swim, I guess."

Benji took off his coat, t-shirt and shoes and stood at the edge of the pool.

"Be careful, Benji!" Flo was tightening her fists now.

"Trust me, I'm a pro!"

Benji dived in; he loved wild swimming. Next to tree climbing, it was his favourite thing to do.

The water was cool and, underneath the surface, it was like another world. Benji swam down to some large rocks and giant mushrooms swaying on the sandy bottom. The warmth of the sunlight pierced though the crevice in the cave above and warmed Benji's skin. At the very bottom of the pool lay the sword, encrusted with coloured jewels.

Benji tried to pick it up, but it would not budge. It seemed so heavy, yet it wasn't lodged in anything. He tried again but he didn't have the strength, so he swam back to the surface. He sprang out of the water and took a deep breath. "It's too heavy," he said panting. "I just can't seem to budge it!"

"Let's go," said Flo as the light from above began to wane.

"One more go…"

Benji took a deep breath and dived into the depths. This time the water was colder and murkier.

Benji thought he could see something out of the corner of his eye. Like a tail, darting behind a rock.

8
SWORD OF STONES

Flo peered into the water of the pool while Star barked wildly and growled at the edge of the water. Seconds later, she saw it. A huge snake was sneaking through the water, coiling its way in and out of the rocks. Its body had the thickness of a tree trunk and its scales were black.

"Benji!" she screamed.

Flo could see Benji reaching for the sword at the bottom of the pool. He gripped it with both hands and pulled, but it did not move. Approaching from behind, the monstrous snake wrapped its thick body around him and tried to carry him away, but Benji did not let go of the sword. With one big pull, he yanked it from the ground.

Star began to howl.

The next moment, the ground trembled and a blinding light flashed up through the water, creating rainbows everywhere. The entire cave shook as Flo and Star huddled together by the edge of pool. The snake lifted Benji, with the sword still in his hands, up and out of the water. Benji gasped for breath as the serpent squeezed him in a tight knot and lifted him high into the air, twisting its body in a death roll in the shadows.

The snake rose to the top of the cave, its eyes glowing a deep green colour, its sharp teeth and black forked tongue rattling and hissing. Its long black body writhed and whipped the water, drenching Flo and Star who were hiding behind a big rock.

"Flo!" Benji cried as he was thrashed about in the air.

"I'm here!" she replied.

Benji hurled the rainbow sword towards her and she lurched forward to grab hold of it. But when she gripped the handle, it was too heavy to lift. Flo looked up and caught sight of the light of the moon seeping through a crack in the wall of the cave. As it hit her, she began to glow. She felt a strange calm take hold of her.

Suddenly, a surge of light shot up from the ground and through her feet like a million moonbeams. She felt so much taller. She held onto the sword, which now filled her arms with a new strength. The weapon started to swing in the air with an energy and force that didn't belong to her. She was radiant, full of a power not her own.

The snake shot towards her while swinging Benji in the air. He started to make choking sounds as its grip tightened around his waist. Then the snake lowered its head to the ground and opened its mouth, ready to swallow Flo. But Flo was emboldened now. Whatever power was working in her gave her the strength to lift the sword high into the air. Each tiny stone shone as the light poured from Flo's body. With one mighty slash, she brought the blade down across the snake's neck, cutting off its head.

Benji fell back into the water with a splash. He swam to the side and crawled out of the pool, catching his breath. Flo and Star stood staring at the head of the gigantic snake. Thick black blood oozed from its gaping neck across the wet ground. Flo ran to Benji while and Star licked his face.

Just then, both children stared in horror as what looked like hundreds of scorpions appeared from the snake's neck and started scuttling with the flow of the serpent's blood into the dark crevices of the cave.

"You did it! You saved me!" Benji cried.

"This sword has a mind of its own!" Flo said.

Benji took hold of the sword. It did not seem so heavy anymore. The handle was encrusted with tiny stones in all the colours of the rainbow. At the centre of the handle was a bright red ruby set in a golden sun, and the long blade itself was like a diamond, shimmering in pinks, purples and blues. It was sharp on both edges and as clear as the water in the pool when they arrived. Benji and Flo were stunned. It was as though the colour carried a power of its own. A light and gentle sound emanated from it, a sound like singing.

As the cave filled with bright light, the children had to cover their eyes. When they opened them, they saw thousands of butterflies grouping together just like they had done in Flo's dream. Once again, they morphed into the shape of the Moon Queen. Her broad wings filled the chamber. Her gentle voice sounded like a flowing stream. She was brilliant and lyrical, clothed in the light of the moon.

"Well done, children," she said. The bright lady bowed low towards Benji and Flo. "I am the Moon Queen. You have both shown great courage and for this you will be rewarded." As she spoke, her long golden hair fell like flames from beneath her golden diadem, adorned with twisting leaves and thorns.

Flo bowed but the bright Queen smiled and pulled her up by the hand. "You are the daughter of the Fire King. I am simply a messenger of his light. I bow to you, not you to me."

"Flo saved us!" Benji said, looking down at the ground.

"Yes, she did," the Moon Queen said with a smile.

Flo blushed. She had never felt so brave.

"But two are more powerful than one, Benji," the Moon Queen added. "Flo needed to cut off the beast's head to find her courage, but it was you who brought her here to crush her fear in the first place."

Benji blushed.

"But this is just a test. There are more battles to be had against the Shadow Prince in Battlelands. The war is fierce."

As the Moon Queen spoke, it was as though she grew brighter with every word.

"Don't forget, if it had not been for the python's grip in the depths of the water, you would not have pulled out the sword. Shadows cannot be cast without light."

"Who is the Shadow Prince?" asked Benji.

"He seeks to steal the soul of every Fire Child. He is the one taking the life and colour from your world."

"Why doesn't the Fire King destroy him?" Flo asked.

"That's a good question. Colour must return to your world first. It is through you, the King's Fire Children, that this must happen."

Benji frowned.

"The Fire King has chosen well," the Queen said before drawing close to Benji and Flo. Her glowing hand touched their heads. When it did, it was as if a million moonbeams filled their bodies and they shone like stars.

After that, a heaviness fell upon them and they closed their eyes. What seemed like only seconds later, they woke up at the foot of their tree at the Old Hall. They sat up and rubbed their eyes. The sky was grey. Everything was black and white again.

"Did that really happen?" Flo asked as she shuddered and looked down at her porcelain white arms.

"Where's the light?" Benji asked. The blue light and the steps inside the tree had disappeared.

The friends sat, taking in what they had just experienced. Then Benji reached into his pocket and pulled out two ginger cookies. He handed one to Flo, who giggled. "You always have a stash!" She snapped hers in half and gave some to Star.

They sat beneath the oak tree and nibbled their biscuits. The sky was beginning to darken, so they knew they had not been away long, even though it had felt like hours in the cave. It seemed like a dream, and yet the box, the mandolin and the scroll were still in the hollow of the tree and Benji's clothes were still damp from the water in the blue pool. Most of all, the sword of stones was still fixed in his hand.

It was then that they noticed that the handle of the sword had been engraved with a name.

Florence Knightly.

Benji passed the sword to Flo. She gripped it in her right hand and felt brave again. Although the sword no longer had the rainbow colours they had seen in the cave, it still sparkled like a great diamond.

She lifted the flat of the blade to her ear.

It was still singing.

9
MONKEYS

The branches of the trees in Witch Wood shook as a strong wind swept the autumn leaves up from the ground. Some of the old leaves crunched beneath Benji's feet as he strolled to school. He was feeling glum. Weeks had passed since Flo and he had been in the cave. Nothing unusual had occurred since they last talked with the Moon Queen. As he stared up at the whirling sky, Benji longed for another adventure. He didn't like the fact that everything had returned to normal. He was even starting to wonder whether the pool and the serpent had been a crazy dream.

As Benji was lost in his thoughts, a large conker hit his head. When he lowered his gaze, he saw hundreds of conkers in their spiky grey cases scattered all around his feet beneath the horse-chestnut tree. Just as he was thinking it was an accident, another conker flew horizontally towards him. He ducked and it passed over his head. It was then that he saw Ozzy Stone. His short, muscular build was unmistakable. He was a super-fast runner and not a bad climber either.

"Watch yourself, Brooksy!" he shouted. "These conkers might knock you out!"

"Benji!" Flo called from halfway down the path, carrying five big, heavy library books under one arm and waving a piece of paper in the other.

"Get lost!" Benji warned Ozzy, just as he was about to lob a conker back at him. Flo caught up with them and her presence defused the situation.

"Aww, your girlfriend is here to save you!"

"She's not my girlfriend…"

"Poor little Brooksy needs a girl to save him!"

Benji picked up a shiny conker and threw it towards Ozzy. Ozzy, anticipating the move, hid behind the tree and laughed.

"Get lost, Stone!"

Ozzy jumped from behind the tree and startled Flo, who dropped her books. Benji picked up another conker but Ozzy was running up the path. He was almost as fast as a whippet and disappeared in the distance.

"You just watch it, Stone!" Benji shouted. "One of these days I will…"

"Stop it!" Flo didn't like seeing Benji angry because when he lost his temper, he really lost it. His cheeks would blaze with rage.

"One of these days I will hurl a conker right between his eyes and knock him out!" Benji's eyes looked as if they might pop out of his head. He grabbed a few big conkers and shoved them in his pockets.

"Don't be too hard on him." Flo's eyes widened. "My mum says Ozzy is an orphan. His mother ran away when he was a baby and never came back. Then his dad drank himself to death, and he's now left with his grumpy uncle. Mum says he's not capable of raising a child. For a while he even went into foster care, but he was so badly behaved no one wanted him. In the end, his uncle took him back, but he did a poor job of looking after him. That's why Ozzy steals the apples from the school tree for his breakfast, because Mr Stone would forget to feed him. Some say Mr Stone has never smiled in his whole life and he's been grey since the day he was born!"

"Well, I'm not feeling sorry for him!" Benji said as he stormed up the path, leaving Flo to pick up the big books.

"I wanted to show you my picture of the Moon Queen!" Flo shouted as she waved a piece of paper in the air.

"It wasn't a Moon Queen!" Benji shouted back at her. "It was just a stupid dream!" "We have the sword of stones under my bed!" Flo shouted, curling her fists.

"What sword?" Benji was spitting mad, kicking the leaves as he walked.

When Benji reached the school gates at the end of Witch Wood path, the wind was now thrashing the trees. He was so enraged that he failed to spot the shadow of a monkey jumping from tree to tree above his head and darting across the roof of the school.

When he entered the school, there was an air of excitement in the corridors. The next day was Halloween and many of the children at Kingswick Primary School were looking forward to the Spooky Disco. Benji and Flo had become more and more uneasy about celebrating Halloween since their meeting with the tall dark figure and their battle with the giant python. The darkness felt more real to them now.

As the bell rang, the children swept through the double doors.

"Order! Order!" Mrs Electra shrieked as she stood in front of the stampeding children. Her hands were placed firmly on her hips. Her hair rose like a mountain on her head and her dark eyes were fierce. The children slowed down before her and parted like the Red Sea to avoid her. All, that is, except Ozzy Stone, the only child who didn't seem scared of Mrs Electra in the slightest.

"One at a time, Oswald Stone!" Mrs Electra spat at Ozzy as she shouted.

"Urgh!" Ozzy screeched. "That's gross!"

He ran straight to the boys' toilets to wash his face.

Benji sniggered as Mrs Electra stared at him over her large glasses. "Tie!" she shouted. Benji rolled his eyes and adjusted his tie. He hated the feeling of being strangled, but the teacher insisted. To him, it felt like a noose.

The children waded into class as Mr Crouch was writing on the whiteboard. *The Raven, by Edgar Allen Poe*. Mr Crouch sat at the edge of his desk, tapping his pen as he stared the children into silence. Then he started to read. *Once upon a midnight dreary, while I pondered, weak and weary...*

Ozzy already had his head in his hands and eyes his were closing. Mr Crouch continued to recite the poem and then thumped the table. Ozzy jumped. He was roused from his trance to find Mr Crouch staring at him. His voice grew louder and louder as he became more and more enthused with the poem. Ozzy yawned again.

Mr Crouch, who was a tall gangly man with a face like a coffee pot, turned to the whiteboard and began to highlight the repetitive sounds in the poem with his pen. Benji pulled out a big shiny conker from the deep of his pocket and lobbed it at the back of Ozzy's head.

"Ouch!" he cried. Ozzy looked down to see the conker rolling towards Mr Crouch's thin pointy shoes.

The teacher picked up the missile and looked straight at Ozzy with his small black eyes.

"What is this?"

"Benji threw it! It wasn't me!"

"It wasn't me!" Benji cried. Flo looked at him disapprovingly from the other side of the classroom. Benji blushed.

"Throwing conkers in my classroom! You silly senseless, idiotic child." Ozzy's cheeks grew darker.

"Oswald Stone and Benjamin Brook, you will stay behind at break and we will get to the bottom of this. This will also give us more time to discuss the works of Poe in more depth and detail!"

The bell rang and the children jumped out of their seats to go, all except for Benji and Ozzy, who were flashing angry looks at one another. But just as Benji was planning his next move, he was startled by what he saw on Ozzy's shoulders. There, looking back at him with dark beady eyes, was what appeared to be a little black monkey. Benji blinked and rubbed his eyes. The monkey sat with its legs wrapped around Ozzy's neck and its head resting on top of his skull, making the boy look as if he had two heads. The creature put its hands over Ozzy's ears and stared back at Benji with the most hideous smile he had ever seen. Its teeth were like dominoes and its tongue was grey. Then the monkey screeched and shook Ozzy's head from side to side.

Mr Crouch looked at Ozzy with concern. "Are you alright, Oswald? You have gone ghastly pale."

"I feel sick, sir!"

Just then, the monkey leapt from Ozzy and jumped at Benji who almost jumped out of his skin. He hid behind his desk trembling.

"What on earth are you doing?" Mr Crouch hollered from the front of the classroom.

"The monkey!" Benji squealed. "It's going to get me!"

"What monkey? Are you boys playing a trick? I will be sending you to Mr van Hoff's office if you don't sit back down immediately!"

Benji climbed back into his chair. The monkey was crouching by the window looking at him with impish eyes. It opened its mouth and made a strange rattling sound. Then five more monkeys started crawling along the walls of the classroom and jumping across the desks. They whizzed past Mr Crouch, making the small tuft of hair at the back of his head twitch. Mr Crouch looked around suspiciously and scratched his head.

"I threw the conker and I am really sorry," Benji said. He just wanted to get out of there as soon as possible. His anger towards Ozzy was disappearing. The more he realized there was an entirely different battle going on, the more his hatred subsided.

"Very well. I will be keeping an eye on the pair of you. What do you have to say to Oswald?"

"Sorry Ozzy," Benji whimpered. It wasn't easy showing mercy to a boy like Ozzy Stone, but for the first time in his life he felt quite sorry for him, what with the horrible monkey tormenting him.

As soon as Benji said sorry, the monkeys shrieked and then shot through the glass windowpane and vanished.

"Can I go?" Ozzy asked.

"Yes go, both of you. You have a black card each. If I have any more trouble, you will be sent to Mr van Hoff's office. Understood?"

"Yes, Mr Crouch," they both said, leaving the classroom.

"It's not over yet," hissed Ozzy.

Benji ignored him and ran off to the library to look for Flo. He found her sitting on a beanbag with her head buried in a large book about snakes in the Amazon rainforest. Benji grabbed a random book about human anatomy on his way. The librarian peered sternly over her glasses at Benji.

"I'm sorry," whispered Benji. "I do believe it. I don't really know why I said I didn't. I was a jerk. Ozzy Stone just makes my blood boil."

"I forgive you," said Flo, and Benji collapsed into a beanbag by her side, ready to tell her about the monkeys.

"Look at this," Flo whispered as she pointed to a huge snake. "This is a black anaconda, which means 'good swimmer' in Greek. It's from South America, one of the largest snakes in the world, like the one that almost squeezed you to death."

"I've got something important to tell you Flo. It's not about snakes." Benji often had to break Flo out of her stream of thought. "I saw five shadow monkeys in Mr Crouch's classroom!"

Flo shut her book.

"One jumped on top of Ozzy's head and then they all vanished through the window when I apologised to him!"

Flo was all ears now.

10

THE SPOOKY DISCO

Flo lay curled up on the sofa with Star snuggling beside her. White flames danced in the open fire, making them as warm as toast. Star's paws trembled as she made little yelping sounds while she slept. Flo smiled and wondered if she was dreaming of wide-open spaces and flying sticks.

"It's the Spooky Disco in less than an hour, Flo." Flo's dad had just entered the sitting room. "It's time for you and Bea to get ready."

Flo sighed. She had lost all enthusiasm for the disco; the thought of dressing up as the White Witch didn't really appeal to her anymore. But as she stared into the waning fire, an idea popped into her mind. Her white dress and icicle tiara would turn her into a fine Moon Queen! She jumped to her feet and scampered upstairs.

Forty minutes later, the bell rang. Mr Knightly opened the door to find little Jo dressed in a skeleton onesie and Benji as a bat, with a mandolin in hand. He wore black cut-off trousers, a grey vest with the Batman symbol on his chest, and a black eye mask.

"Well!" gasped Mrs Knightly as she joined her husband at the door. "Don't you look a picture! What are you?"

"Batman, of course!" Benji said as he stretched his arms out and a large pair of black, elastic wings extended either side of him.

"Ah! I see. You look...very convincing."

As Benji shrieked like a bat and waved his mandolin in the air, Mrs Knightly put her hands over her ears.

Mr Knightly looked stern. He seemed to get irritated every time Mrs Knightly did anything dramatic.

"And here is the White Witch and the pumpkin," he said, standing aside to show Bea and Flo leaning against the warm radiator in the hallway. Bea was dressed as a large, grey round pumpkin and Flo wore a long white dress, a sparkling tiara and the sword of stones in a belt across her back.

Benji smiled and said, "You look just like the Moon Queen!"

"That's the idea."

"Where did you get that sword, Flo?" asked Mrs Knightly.

Flo looked to the ground and clenched her fists.

"We found it!" Benji said, butting in.

Thankfully, no more questions were asked. It seemed Flo's mum and dad assumed that the weapon was a toy and Flo was relieved that she didn't have to lie. She didn't know how to lie. She hated lying and she wasn't quite sure if her mum would believe her if she told the truth.

"I don't want you walking home tonight. I will come and get you," Mrs Knightly said.

"Jen, the disco finishes at 9pm," Mr Knightly said. "It's literally around the corner. They'll be perfectly safe."

"I insist on collecting them, Tom. Times have changed. Even in Kingswick, bad things can happen."

"It's a stone's throw away, Jen. Honestly, you're being ridiculous."

"I will pick you up at 9pm." Mrs Knightly stood with her hands on her hips, staring at her husband.

"We'd better go, or we'll be late. We'll be at the gates at 9pm, Mum," Flo said as she looked at Benji, hoping her parents would stop their bickering.

"Now stay together!" Mrs Knightly said. "It's your responsibility to look after Bea and Jo at the disco, both of you."

Benji nodded and tousled Jessie's blonde hair. Jo showed his pretend fangs and tried to make a creepy noise, but he looked too cute and cuddly to be scary.

"We will."

Flo giggled and held onto Bea's hand, but her heart was heavy as she shut the door. She could hear Mr and Mrs Knightly continuing their quarrel.

As they wandered towards school, taking the long way, the stars were plentiful and the moon looked as though it was swelling in the sky. Flo shuddered at the thought of walking through Witch Wood during Halloween.

As the children approached the school gates, they were greeted by a ghoulish sight, made even more ghostly now that everything was in black and white. Children were dressed as devils and witches, holding buckets of sweets and toffee apples. Swollen, ignited pumpkin heads carved with sharp teeth and triangular eyes lined the path towards double doors festooned with spiders' webs.

Just as they were about to go into the school hall, Ozzy Stone jumped in front of them and Flo, Jo and Bea stepped back, hiding behind Benji. Ozzy was dressed as a vampire with a white painted face and fake black blood dripping from his eyes and mouth.

"What the heck are you?" Ozzy asked as he looked Benji up and down. "Hey everyone, check out Benji Brook."

A gang of vampires and grim reapers laughed and pointed.

"Since when did batman play the violin?" Ozzy was laughing hysterically now.

"It's not a violin, stupid! It's a mandolin."

"Ignore him, Benji," Flo said, her fists tightening. Then she shouted, "Toffee apples!"

Benji spun on his heels. The delicious smell drew him away to a stall with apples dipped in chocolate, dripping toffee and black-and-white sprinkles.

As the sound system blasted out the tune to Ghostbusters, the hall filled with hundreds of children in Halloween costumes. Jo and Bea skipped off with their Reception class friends. Meanwhile, Benji and Flo gravitated towards the year 5 and 6's and enjoyed dancing, eating cupcakes decorated with pumpkin smiles and black bats, and drinking frothy hot chocolate.

Joanna Woods wheeled over to them and dressed as a black fairy, her and Flo danced to the music. Joanna spun her chair in circles and Flo danced around her.

After several songs, Flo looked around and realised that Benji had disappeared.

"Back soon," she said to Joanna as she set off down the dark, quiet corridors in search of her friend.

The school felt freakish in the nighttime. There was a chill in the air and tall shadows slivered up the walls. As she searched further away from the school hall, she didn't notice Ozzy Stone and a grim reaper following.

When Flo peered into Mr Crouch's room, she found Benji sat in the dark on the windowsill looking up at the moon.

"What are you doing in here?"

"Looking for the shadow monkeys."

"Why?"

"They might lead us to Battlelands."

Flo walked towards the window and they both peered up at the wide moon in the dark sky. Little did they know that Ozzy Stone and his grim reaper friend were just outside the door, listening to every word they were saying.

11
CAST

Ozzy's dark eyes narrowed, as he strained his ears as close to door as he could without being seen. He pressed his body against the wall as he squinted to a point where he was almost cross-eyed.

Just then, a glowing white butterfly flew through the doorway.

"Rainbow!" Flo cried.

Ozzy gawped as Rainbow flew like a little fairy light into the dark classroom and straight towards Benji and Flo. Then she fluttered through the window and vanished into the night.

"We must go into Witch Wood," Benji said.

"No way! It will be really dark, and we can't leave Jo and Bea behind!"

"They are safe in the hall with the teachers. We must follow Rainbow."

Ozzy and his grim reaper buddy remained hidden as Flo and Benji left the room.

"Did you see what I just saw?"

"See what?"

"That butterfly."

"You've drunk too much fizz. Come on, Oz. We're missing all the fun!" The grim reaper ran off down the corridor towards the hall, but Ozzy lingered. Something weird was going on and he wanted to know what Benji Brook was up to.

Ozzy followed Benji and Flo outside towards the gates at Witch Wood. Flo was right; heading into Witch Wood was petrifying at nighttime. Even Benji looked scared as the moon appeared to shine brighter in the sky and a silvery light pierced through the thick trees to illuminate the path. The forest was filled with all sorts of strange sounds as they walked deeper into the trees. There was a breeze and they could hear leaves crunching and twigs snapping, which made them jump and look behind into the shadows.

Ozzy remained at a safe distance, lurking behind a tree every time they looked around. His heart was thumping, and his mouth was dry. He was beginning to regret following them.

"Look!" Flo whispered, her voice just loud enough for Ozzy to hear. "Can you see that light?"

They shuffled closer to a mysterious light source to discover a moon-like orb swirling in white light. The orb was about eight feet high and shone like a star. It looked as if it had landed on the path and was now ablaze like a bonfire.

Ozzy could feel the heat from it as he hid behind the horse-chestnut tree. His heart was beating so loudly now that he was sure they would hear it. He took a step backwards. A twig snapped.

"Who's there?" Benji asked.

Ozzy froze.

"I said, who's there?"

"W-w-w-what's going on?" Ozzy blurted as he emerged from behind the tree.

"What are you doing here, Ozzy?" Benji shouted.

"What's this?" Ozzy said, trying to conceal his fear. "What trick are you pulling, Brooksy?"

"This isn't a trick. It's real."

"What you on about?"

Just then, the orb began to move towards Ozzy who fell back and shrieked. Then the orb began to speak.

"Don't be afraid."

The bright, ball of light morphed into a tall male figure with wide, feathered wings. The figure stood about eight feet tall and his hair flowed in golden fiery locks. His torso and arms were muscular and bronze and there was a golden armlet in the shape of a lion's head curled around his bicep. He had fastened a golden belt around his waist above a bronze chain-metal skirt. His feet were bare.

"My name is Cast," he said with a smile. "I am a star."

The bronze-winged man walked over to Ozzy and crouched low beside him. His eyes were fiery blue. He lowered his head in a bow towards Ozzy, then he touched the boy's arm. Ozzy's body began to feel warm.

Cast looked deep into Ozzy's eyes. Ozzy was shocked to see tears fall to the ground like moonlit pearls.

"The Shadow Prince stole your mother," Cast said, still bowing low. It was as though he could look deep into Ozzy's heart and see everything.

"I don't have a mother," Ozzy said, trying to be obstinate.

Cast stood tall and raised his wings. He moved them to and fro while a light wind swept across him.

"You are not an orphan, Ozzy. You belong to the King."

At the mention of the King, there was a loud shrieking in the sky.

"It is time for battle," Cast said.

"What battle?" asked Ozzy. He was shaking.

"Stay together and you will succeed. The Shadow Prince is afraid when the Fire Children unite. He would rather keep you scattered."

The strange creature looked up into the night sky then back at the children. "Come quickly! The harpies are close."

Right on cue, there was an ear-piercing screech and seven dark figures with long black hair and leathery wings swooped down like witches. They cawed in the darkness like giant crows as they stared at the children with their deep black eyes.

"He belongs to us!" one shrieked, her black hands reaching out for Ozzy from under her wings. Ozzy ran to Cast and hid in his light. No sooner had he taken refuge there than the light from his protector poured into him. Ozzy felt stronger. Braver.

Cast roared like a lion at the harpies, whose eyes turned from greed to fear. They scattered across the sky, like howling street cats in a late-night fight.

"It's time," said Cast, as he scooped up Benji, Flo and Ozzy in his wings. He lifted them from the ground and moved so fast everything became a white blur of light. The next moment, the children were standing by the window of the school hall. They watched with horror as the children inside screamed at the seven harpies circling above them.

"Get them!" they cackled as they swooped down.

The children at the window stared in helpless agony as the bat-like monsters dived down and snatched Jo, Bea and Joanna from the ground with their sharp black claws.

All they left behind was Joanna's silver chair.

12

BATTLELANDS

Ozzy began to back away from the window. "Get me out of here!" he cried. Flo, who was staring up into the sky, was crying. Her flooded eyes were peering up into the night, following the harpies who were carrying her friends away.

"No! We must save them!" Benji said.

"Remember," Cast said. "The Shadow Prince is afraid of unity. Stay together and sing for strength." There was a rumble in his voice, like the sound of distant thunder.

Flo began to hum their song and Benji started to play the mandolin.

Ozzy's face twisted. "What are you freaks doing?" He continued to shuffle backwards and fell to the ground.

Cast burst into a blazing ball of fire. His light was so bright the children covered their eyes. Cast's fireball spun like a tornado as Benji and Flo stepped forward into the light…

"Wait!" Ozzy cried. He launched himself forwards with his arms outstretched towards Flo as her body was swallowed up in the light. As soon as Ozzy's hand touched the light, his body filled with warmth again and he glowed like the moon in the sky. In one deep breath, he stepped forward and found himself spinning in the tunnel of light as it twisted upwards and away into the black sky.

Within a few seconds, Ozzy was no longer in Kingswick but standing in a wide-open field. A gigantic moon filled the starry sky. It felt like nighttime, except that everything was bathed in a golden light. The moon must have been ten times the size of the one back home.

Benji and Flo stood beneath it, their bodies lit up in its golden glow. A meadow of colourful grass stretched out in front of them for miles. Each blade was different in colour – purples, pinks, blues, and every shade of green. Each grew like wildflowers as far as their eyes could see. Everything was calm.

"Look at all the colour," Ozzy gasped.

"Ozzy!" Benji said.

"Your eyes!" Ozzy cried. "They're blue! And your hair … it looks like lightning!"

Ozzy stretched out his hands to see his own skin was no longer grey but a warm chestnut colour again.

"Your hair's all black and wiry, Ozzy," Benji said. "It's sticking up. And your eyes… they're ebony."

Ozzy looked at Flo and his heart fluttered. "Flo, your eyes are like dark chocolate. Your hair's gone all brown."

Flo's skin was porcelain white, with a slight peach hue in her cheeks. Ozzy thought she looked quite beautiful, glowing in the moonlight.

With the air being so warm, winter in Kingswick felt a world away. The silver clouds above seemed to scud at unusual speed. Tiny orbs of light the size of marbles danced above them, and the sound of childlike voices filled the air. The songs were so beautiful it made the children's hair stand on end. The gentle rain sparkled like silver glitter as it rested on their skin and moistened the ground.

What looked like a diamond with speckled wings flew in front of

Ozzy's face. His eyes blurred. Flo held out her hands and cupped it from the air, as if scooping a glassy shrimp from a seaside pool. She took a closer look. A creature like a golden firefly shone in her hands. It was the same size and shape as a diamond in an engagement ring, except that the glass was filled with liquid fire. It had silver, mottled wings, a tiny tail, and a face like a caterpillar. Ozzy felt drawn to its bulging black eyes.

Just then, a short gold antenna twitched on its head and then its small curved mouth opened. It looked up at them and smiled.

"Hello," said the creature in a soft, childlike voice. As it spoke, the soothing sound of music filled the air. Ozzy could make out something resembling a flute, viola and cello. The riff had a kind of Celtic vibe to it.

Ozzy felt dizzy. "Who are you?" he asked. "W-w-what are you? W-w-where are we?"

"I am Blaze. Very pleased to meet you, Fire Child." The creature bowed his little head. "I am the leader of the fireflies. We are here to guide you to the Black Mountains."

"What is this place? Am I dreaming?" Ozzy's voice was trembling and his body shuddering. "How do we get back? I need to get out of here. It's creepy. I should never have followed you, Benji Brook. It's your fault."

"Don't blame me, Ozzy. You chose to follow us!"

"Stop!" Flo cried. She placed her fists under her chin and looked to the ground. "Cast said we need to stay close and you are not following the rules!"

"We're in the middle of nowhere with a bunch of talking fairies," Ozzy said. "This is weird, and I want to go home!" He thumped his foot on the ground as he finished.

"We are not fairies. We are fireflies! We carry the light of the King and we are very important guides!"

"Is that a piano?" asked Flo, breaking the kerfuffle and staring into the sky at a shape forming above her.

The children gawped at the sky as the sound of music filled the air. Clusters of big stars created amazing shapes. Flo pointed out the Pleiades and Orion, but what they had all never seen before amongst the clusters were so many other shapes – a child, a mandolin, a sword, a man, a key and a door.

As they gazed above them, hundreds of fireflies flew to them and joined in singing in perfect harmony.

Arise, Fire Child
Resolute and wise
Raise your weapons to the skies
Colour will return
To an ashen world
When the Shadow Prince is defied

Arise, Fire Child
Arise, Arise, Arise

"You know the words!" said Flo.

"This is our favourite battle song," Blaze said.

A serious look spread across Flo's face. "We must help rescue my little sister Bea, Benji's little brother Jo, and my best friend Joanna. Do you know where the harpies might have taken them?"

"We can guide you as far as the Black Mountains. It should take us two days, so you might want to wear some comfortable boots."

The children looked down to discover a pair of sturdy silver boots, with gold caps and a brown fur lining in front of them.

"These are your moon boots."

"They're lovely!" Flo said.

"They're weird," Ozzy added.

"These are your boots for battle. Now, let's get you cleaned up and kitted out. You can't wear those silly clothes."

Ozzy sunk his feet into the moon boots. He tried not to show how comfortable they felt. No sooner were they on his feet than he began to glow and float a little from the ground. Flo and Benji put theirs on and they too began to glow like moonbeams.

"This is so cool!" Benji cried as he followed hundreds of fireflies whizzing away. The boots seemed to have some sort of built-in air pressure that helped the children move faster. Ozzy felt a little like an astronaut might on the moon as he bounced off the ground with each stride.

"This way!" Blaze said, as the fireflies shot towards a river in the distance.

13

THE RIVER

When the children arrived at the riverbank, they began to set up camp under a navy sky crammed full of stars. After they had finished, they looked at the reflection of the huge moon shimmering in the quiet flowing river. Benji had the overwhelming urge to jump into the water.

"Shall we swim?" he asked Flo. He was whispering, not wanting Ozzy to hear. Benji couldn't help feeling annoyed that Ozzy had followed them all this way and was now part of their secret adventure. He wanted it to be just him and Flo. He hated the thought that Ozzy would now have the chance to defeat giant sea snakes.

As Benji stared down into the water, he drew back in surprise. His reflection was winking back at him. He crept forward and looked again. Sure enough, his reflection looked back at him and smiled.

"Hey, look! I'm smiling at myself!"

"This is a great place to have an honest conversation with yourself," Blaze said. "Just make sure you listen to the best you."

Benji looked down and said, "Hello." His reflection said, "Hello."

Flo sat beside him gazing at herself too. Her reflection spoke. "The water is lovely. Fancy a swim?"

"Oh, I'm not sure."

"Come for a swim," said Benji's reflection.

"How is this happening?" Flo asked.

"Your reflection can be your friend," Blaze replied. "It's good to take your own advice from time to time. But it's also always wise to ask a trusted advisor, to be on the safe side. We can never fully rely on ourselves. Unless, of course, you begin to see the Fire King looking back at you."

Benji giggled and pulled funny faces at himself. His reflection giggled and pulled funny faces back. He then scanned the line of trees across the river and spotted the best one for climbing. He kicked off his boots, took off his batman vest and dived into the crystal-clear river with a huge splash. He swam across and pulled himself up on the other side where a marvellous looking tree with thick, low branches hung over the surface of the water. Benji gripped the bark of the trunk with his bare feet and hands. Just as he was about to climb, he was startled by a deep muffled voice.

"Excuse me! That's my eye you're poking, and your big toe is in my mouth!"

Benji leapt to the ground in horror. The tree trunk he was trying to climb had a face and it was talking to him.

"If you insist on climbing me, would you please try to not step on my face?"

"Oh, I'm sorry. In my world, the trees don't have faces."

"I wouldn't be so sure of that. Feel free to swing from my branches."

"Thanks," Benji said. He was still finding it hard to believe he was talking to a tree. He clambered up with both hands onto the longest branch, coiled himself upwards and then shuffled along the branch. Once over the water, he jumped down into the river with a resounding splash.

Flo took off her moon boots. "Are you coming for a paddle?" she asked Ozzy, as she made her way down a muddy slope to a small stretch of red sand.

Ozzy shook off his boots and wandered over to Flo, who was now paddling in the river. He stood by the edge and watched his face in the rippling water. His face went pale. The peace he had felt when wearing the moon boots evaporated. He sat on the sand and looked up into the night. The moon seemed to spin like a wheel across the sky.

"It's lovely and warm," Flo said.

"I'm feeling sick," said Ozzy as he lay back on the ground.

A firefly flew over to him. "We have just the thing for that! I'm Spark, pleased to meet you."

The little creature wore tiny spectacles. His body contained a shiny liquid, amber in colour, and his delicate wings had sage green stripes.

"The trees that line the river grow leaves to heal ailments and diseases. We have miles of healing trees that stretch right across the land."

He flew to a tall tree growing by the water's edge. The roots of its tall trunk sunk deep beneath the riverbed. Its leaves were emerald green with glowing, golden berries hanging around and beneath them.

"I need a strong leaf to calm the nerves," Spark said as he fluttered to the top of the tree.

A deep slow voice came from the tree. "Top left. The rattlers have been nibbling away on those. I think you'll find they are the most medicinal."

"Thank you, Trebador."

"You're welcome."

Trebador's trunk had sunken eyes, a nose, ears and a mouth that you could easily miss if you weren't observant enough. Its weathered face was old and wrinkled with dark brown mossy bark. When Spark plucked the sage green leaf with tiny nibbled holes, Trebador closed his eyes and fell asleep again, snoring heavily.

"Thank you," Spark said as he took the sage green leaf and the amber fire berries to Ozzy and dropped them into his lap. "Eat them," he said. "It will relieve your shock. Chew them up and you will be as right as silver rain."

"I'm not eating that!"

"Of course you are!" Spark chirped. "They will make you feel better. They aren't easy to come by, you know."

Just then, another firefly flew over. "Have them in a drink," she said,

"Better if you chew them," Spark interrupted.

"Yes, but the Fire Child is feeling sensitive."

"All right, Flick, hand it over..."

Flick, who had a similar colouring to Spark, took the leaf and berries from Ozzy's hand and plopped them in a round wooden bowl filled with warm water. The berries were filled with what looked like swirling, sizzling flames. A delicious smelling steam tickled Ozzy's nose.

"Drink," she said, fluttering close to his face.

Ozzy squinted and winced as he held the cup with his shaky hands. He still looked a ghastly pale. He felt reluctant, but it did smell sweet.

Ozzy took a sip.

The delicious warm water slipped down his throat and a soothing calm filled his eyes. It felt different from what the children had experienced putting on the moon boots – deeper, heavier, dreamier.

Ozzy lay back on the multi-coloured grass. Still wearing his vampire costume, he started to relax. Then he fell asleep.

Meanwhile, Benji and Flo were splashing around in the river. They eventually climbed out of the water and put on the clothes the fireflies had laid out for them. Benji was given a bright turquoise hoodie, which made his eyes look even bluer. He wore khaki combats and a brown leather belt with a loop to carry a weapon.

"I'm so glad to take this thing off," Flo said, taking off her Moon Queen dress. "It's rather itchy and not very practical." She then put on a silver hoodie with a soft fleece lining. It had pretty, golden leaves embroidered on it.

"These are so comfortable!" she said, slipping on her rainbow coloured leggings.

"These are the boys' weapons that will help ward off the shadows," Blaze said, pointing to a large dagger and a spear laid out on the grass. The silver spear was tall and slender with a golden arrowhead. The dagger was curved like a crescent moon. It was golden and sharp, and the handle had a large red ruby set into a bronze sun.

"The dagger belongs to Ozzy and the spear belongs to you, Benji."

Benji spun in circles like an excited dog. "Whoa! Really? This is for me?"

Benji picked up the spear and stroked its golden point. His name, *Benjamin Brook*, was engraved into the sliver pole. He gripped the weapon and swivelled it around above his head. He felt very important and powerful, ready to defeat any dark beast that would dare come near him. He threw the spear towards a clump of sand. As it hurtled through the air, its golden tip burst into a fiery flame, lighting up the darkness.

"Awesome!" he said.

"And the sword of stones belongs to you, Flo," Blaze said, keeping a safe distance from Benji.

Flo smiled.

"We heard about your battle in the caves against the great sea snake!" Blaze said as a cluster of fireflies flew all around her, making beautiful sounds. "The fairies told us all about it. You were very brave."

"Fairies?" Flo and Benji said at the same time. Benji came to a standstill. His eyes were fiery in the glow of the flaming spear.

"The way you cut off the snake's head in one slice was a cause for great celebration here in Battlelands!"

Flo blushed and took hold of her sword, which was shimmering in every colour of the rainbow.

Benji grinned at Flo as he began to stride like a warrior, slicing the air.

"Come! Eat and sleep!" Blaze said, leading them to a campfire nearby.

Benji and Flo ate sweet berry bread and drank thick hot chocolate as the fireflies sang and played the battle song. A wonderful warmth filled their bodies.

Then they both yawned at the same time.

They curled up by the river and, while the wood in the fire crackled, they both fell into a deep sleep.

14
BAD DREAMS

A blood-orange sun filled the sky as Flo roused from her sleep the next morning. All around her, she could hear the music of the fireflies. She sat up and rubbed her blurry eyes as the trees lining the river waved back at her and smiled. Benji was already awake and walked over to her with a tray of breakfast.

"The breakfast is delicious. Especially the moon muffins!" he said.

Benji looked over at Ozzy, who was still in a deep sleep a few feet away. "We can't trust Ozzy," he whispered in her ear.

Flo's heart fluttered like Rainbow's wings.

"What do you mean?"

"Like I said. I don't think we can trust him."

"Tell me one good reason."

"He's on the Shadow Prince's side."

Flo felt a pain in her tummy as she clenched her fists. "The Moon Queen and Cast both told us to stay together," she said. The twisting in her gut was so painful now that she had to stand. Then, unable to endure it any longer, she ran from Benji towards the riverbank where she sat down, her head in her hands.

Benji scowled as he looked over at Ozzy, who was still asleep.

However, the breakfast tray beside him was enticing, as the delicious smell of fire berry tea filled his nostrils. He picked up his moon muffin – a large hunk of white, chocolate-chipped fluffy bread in the shape of a moon. He sank his teeth into the soft warm scone. His eyes widened and his toes curled as the delicious taste of melted marshmallow, honeycomb chocolate and fire berry jam oozed out of the middle. After just one mouthful, he knew he had to tell Flo about his dream. In fact, he wasn't sure why he didn't tell her in the first place. There had been a niggling thought at the back of his mind that told him to keep it to himself, but the marvellous moon muffin made him so happy he now felt very differently.

"Wait!" he called out to Flo. "This moon muffin is awesome!" His words were distorted as the muffin's contents oozed out of the sides of his mouth.

When Benji reached her, he sat down beside Flo. "Last night I had a really weird dream," he said with his mouth still full. Some sticky marshmallow was sticking to his top lip like a moustache.

Flo looked at him. "Really?"

"Yes. I saw the trees along the river, shaking in a strong wind. Their eyes were wide and angry. I saw dark monkey shadows swinging from tree to tree, crawling up and down the trunks, bearing their sharp teeth in the moonlight."

Benji wiped his lips before continuing.

"The river was black but there was enough light to see my reflection blink back at me. Then it began to speak."

"What did it say?"

"It said that Ozzy is conspiring with the Shadow Prince and that we can't trust him. Then the face faded and was replaced by a dark figure, the one you described in your other dream. It was wearing a black cloak. A black snake was slithering from his arms."

Benji paused.

"And?"

"I saw the figure take off its hood."

"Who was it?"

"Ozzy."

Flo gasped.

"His face was white, and the black snake had wrapped itself around his head like a turban. Then, as he looked at me, he smiled."

"Hang on a minute," Flo said. "We're being tricked! I had a dream too."

"You too?"

Flo began to speak in a low whisper. "Yes. In my dream, I woke up to find the fire had died. The trees were loud and howling, their faces were angry, and their eyes were fierce. Dark shadows of wild monkeys were swinging from branch to branch."

"Just like in mine!"

"I saw a white orb of light floating towards the river, so I followed it. When I reached the river, I saw my own reflection looking back at me."

Benji was now engrossed.

"My reflection looked very serious. It said, 'Protect yourself. Benji and Ozzy are not to be trusted. They will fight and squabble. If you want to save the children and save the world, you must leave them behind. Leave now and follow the path of whispers.' Just then, my reflection turned into you and Ozzy fighting each other with the spear and dagger. Your faces were contorted, your eyes looked mean."

Benji shuddered.

"Then the image turned into you, looking up at me through the water and saying, 'We can't trust Ozzy. He's on the Shadow Prince's side. Trust me. We can't trust him.' You looked very angry. I shouted 'No!' and I reminded you that Cast said we must stay together! Then I woke up."

Benji sighed.

"Someone's trying to get us to fall out," he said.

Just then, Blaze flew over. "It's just bad dreams, both of you. Don't worry. The darkness likes to cast shadows at this time, especially while you are sleeping, when you are more vulnerable to attack."

"Here. Have a drink," Flick said, passing Flo a warm bowl of fire berry tea.

As she took a sip, a deep calm filled her body. The knot in her tummy unwound itself and the pain in her palms disappeared.

"I'm sorry," said Benji.

"I'm sorry too," replied Flo.

"The dream was so dark and creepy," Benji said. "I think any time we see those monkeys, it's a sign that the Shadow Prince is trying to trick us."

"It seems like he can somehow get inside our minds," Flo said.

Benji looked over at the trees. "In my dream the trees were really spooky, but here they seem so nice."

At that moment, Flash flew over and said, "There are many trees that can be trusted along Tree Pass. But beware, there are a few that have been corrupted by the shadows."

"How can we tell the difference?" Flo asked.

"Just taste the fruit. The fruit from a good tree tastes delicious and you will feel the benefits, but a bad tree's fruit tastes bitter. You will be sure to spit it out and feel quite off colour for some time."

"Is there a cure?" Flo asked.

"Thankfully, there is always a remedy." Just then, Flick fluttered over and nodded in agreement. "Leopald will help you."

"Who's Leopald?" Flo asked.

"He's a silver mottled birch and he grows tiny purple berries with yellow spots. They will cause the sickness to subside as quick as a flash, and they taste delicious. We will come across him along our way."

"We need to get ready, then," Benji said. "It's time we were leaving."

15
THE GOLDEN DAGGER

Just then, Ozzy stirred from his sleep and opened his brown eyes. As he gazed into the sky, he watched the fiery amber sun stretch her arms wide. It reminded him of the wonderful dream he had just had, and his heart felt strangely warm.

In his dream, he saw his bare feet sinking into chalk white sand as he looked out at the black ocean. He held five smooth pebbles in his hand. He began to skim them across the water, and they bounced along a path of moonlight, towards a fiery bird that was flying low along the path towards him.

Star balls spun in the air above the water and then they turned into bright-winged creatures. Each wore a long silver dress made of flowing water. Their silvery wings were transparent, and their long hair was as white as the moon. They smiled at Ozzy as the bird of fire came closer. It looked like a giant eagle with flaming wings.

The eagle swooped low and landed beside Ozzy at the edge of the water. Then it turned into a tall, strong man with bright eyes. His skin was dark, and he had black hair, like Ozzy, but his eyes were ablaze. In fact, they were so bright that Ozzy had to look down. His heart felt like it would crack open. The man held Ozzy's hand and said, "Ozzy, it's time to look up."

Ozzy lifted his gaze. As his eyes adjusted to the flames, he felt a tightness in his chest. He had never known a look of such kindness.

For a while, they skimmed stones together. No words were said. All that could be heard was their laughter, and the pebbles splashing across the surface while fire fish leaped in and out of the water.

Then the man grew taller and taller, his burning frame filling the sky, and the darkness above turned to bloodred. The man of fire took on the appearance of an eagle again. He lifted Ozzy high and they flew far above the dark ocean and into the bright glow of the moon.

Ozzy soon found himself alone at the foot of a climbing path made of precious stones. On either side, there were trees and multi-coloured flowers tilting their heads towards him. Each flower had a face and smiled, while birds in vivid red, yellow and bright blue colours flew above his head in figures of eight. Every flower, tree, creature and even the blades of grass seemed to be singing.

As the song grew, many children appeared, laughing and playing with lions whose manes seemed to be made of fire. Meadows stretched out for miles with stunning trees and vibrant fruits and flowers. Ozzy blinked; he could see otherworldly colours that he had never known before. It was hard to describe them.

The children looked like they were from all over the world. Many carried flags from different countries and were singing in languages Ozzy didn't understand. When the children noticed Ozzy, they waved, and the angels bowed low to the ground. Ozzy's eyes took all this in, and he wanted to cry.

Many rainbows filled the sky and at the end of the ascending path, there was a sapphire blue palace high up on a hill. He climbed the hill and stood before the Moon Queen waiting for him at the foot of the glass steps. When Ozzy reached the top, he fell to his knees and closed his eyes. Although it was all so wonderful, his heart was breaking. He just didn't feel as if he belonged there.

Then, to his amazement, the Moon Queen began to cry. She stooped and her tears felt like warm oil dripping onto his head, filling his body with a warm peace. He looked up at her and he asked, "Why are you crying?"

The Moon Queen smiled, and her eyes flashed with blue flames. "I am a creature of light," she said. "All creatures of light are vessels of the Fire King's love. His heart has broken for you many times, Ozzy."

Ozzy's defences started to crumble.

"His heart has broken for so many children like you, who throughout the ages have been wronged. Every time a child is discarded or hurt, a little of the colour in your world fades away. Slowly but surely, over thousands of years, the colour has been drained from your world. This is the work of the Shadow Prince."

As she mentioned his name, the Moon Queen's eyes flashed with fire and her voice became fierce for a moment.

"But the time is coming – indeed, it's very close – when the Fire King will flood the earth with colour again." The Moon Queen looked to the sky. "There was a time when the world became so wicked that the shadows eclipsed the sun and the sky was covered in darkness. The Fire King knew that the only way to save the world would be to drain the Shadow Prince of all his power. The only way to accomplish that was to let his dark fiends tie him to the trunk of a Manza tree. Constricted to its trunk by the grip of a black python, the wicked fiends poured the milky sap known as black blood from the bark of the tree into the Fire King's mouth, and he died a terrible death. Every tree, flower and living creature almost choked on their own tears that day, but just when it seemed that the earth would die of a broken heart, the King awoke with a fire in his eyes and the skies turned bloodred."

The Moon Queen took Ozzy's chin in her hand and looked into his eyes. "Ozzy, the Fire King has given you and all the Fire Children a part to play in bringing the colour back. Will you help him?"

"Me?" Ozzy's voice was wobbling.

"Yes, you."

With that, the Queen reached out her hand. There was a bright golden dagger in her palm. The blade was shaped like a crescent moon and a large shining ruby was set in the centre of the bronze handle.

Ozzy took it. He stared at it with awe-filled eyes.

"This dagger can cut through diamond," she said. Then she reached out her hand and stroked the side of his face. "You were an orphan, Ozzy, but now you are a Fire Child and the Fire King is very proud of you."

"But I haven't done anything."

"You followed the light, Ozzy. That is all you needed to do." The Moon Queen smiled as she spoke.

Ozzy stood up and the Moon Queen reached out her arms and drew him into her embrace. As soon as Ozzy was enfolded there, he knew that this was no ordinary hug. A million moonbeams shot through his body and he felt more alive and more wonderful than he had ever done. A gust of love, like an avalanche, fell upon him. All the huge, angry feelings he had harboured in his heart began to subside. It was like the boiling lava inside a volcano had suddenly frozen in stone and his rage, once active, was now dormant forever. In that place of unparalleled serenity, Ozzy fell asleep.

It was then that he had awoken.

Now, as he wiped a tear from his eyes, he looked for his former enemies. As he adjusted to the light, he saw a tray of fire berry tea and moon muffins lying beside him. While he drank and ate, the peace within him grew and grew.

A few moments later, he looked up again and saw Benji and Flo walking towards him. They were fully dressed, with their furry moon boots on, and they were clutching their weapons.

Benji handed Ozzy a golden dagger.

"Morning, Ozzy. This belongs to you." Benji was smiling as he spoke.

Ozzy's jaw dropped. "Wow! Thanks. The Moon Queen gave me this same weapon in my dream last night."

Flo and Benji looked at each other and gave a knowing nod. Benji held out his hand and pulled Ozzy to his feet. "I'm sorry for being a jerk," he said.

"Me too," Ozzy said, feeling a bit shy.

Benji looked surprised.

Ozzy looked up at Flo. She looked away and clenched her fists. His heart suddenly filled with a deep ache, and he was surprised to feel a lump in his throat. He tried very hard not to cry but the bubble of sadness grew bigger and bigger inside him. For the first time in his life, he felt so sorry for Flo and for all the children to whom he had been so mean. He thought about Joanna too and then tears began to stream down his cheeks.

"I'm sorry for making fun of you, Flo," he said, wiping the tears away. He lowered his head.

"It's okay," Flo said. She blushed a little and her fists loosened.

The fireflies fluttered all around them playing merry tunes. The faint forms of the creatures of light that Ozzy had seen in his dream appeared behind each one of them. Their translucent wings folded around each child.

"Can you see them?" asked Flo.

"Yes," said Benji.

"I think we just saw angels."

"We did," Ozzy said.

16

BOO

Benji, overwhelmed by his excitement at the prospect of their journey, flipped over in a perfect somersault. When he returned to his feet, he saw three lightning white horses with silver manes and eyes like jasper. They were waiting at the edge of the river at Tree Pass. The three children ran over to the animals and mounted them. Benji leaned forward and hugged the shiny mane. His horse hoofed the ground and snorted.

With the sky a deep violet and the sun high, they trotted on their way, passing hundreds of chattering trees. Every hour or two, the children and the fireflies would stop, rest and refuel, using an array of multi-coloured fruit and leaves they had collected along their way, including Leopold's purple berries with yellow spots.

The Rainbow Tree was the most extraordinary; it didn't look anything like the trees they had seen in their own world, nor even in this world, for that matter. It was medium height with a thick trunk. Growing out of its bark were what looked like little, red, waxy butterfly wings. From its winding golden branches, large gleaming rainbow leaves were flourishing, each the size of a man's hand.

Flash and Flick plucked some rainbow leaves and a few of the red, waxy wings.

"Thank you kindly," Flash said.

"You're very welcome," the tree said.

Flick and Flash took a few large rainbow-coloured leaves and passed them to the children.

"Here," said Flick. "Keep these safe in the pockets of your moon boots. They are a powerful remedy for sickness and disease."

Flash then passed them some of the red, waxy butterfly wings. "These are tree kisses. Squeeze them together like a pair of lips and you will see a sweet resin form. One drop will heal you in no time."

"Wow!" said Benji as he squeezed some resin onto his scuffed knees. Sure enough, the scabs and bruises began to disappear.

"The leaves heal diseases," Flash said, "while the tree kisses soothe pain and draw out any poison. Pop them in your pocket and see."

With that, the group fell silent for a while, until they arrived at a wide-open space. What looked like a crystal white sea stretched out before them.

"That's cool!" exclaimed Benji. "How do we get across?"

"Walk," answered Blaze.

Benji laughed.

"Don't be alarmed," said Blaze. "These are the saltpans. Perfectly fine to walk across."

"I've always wanted to see the salt flats in Bolivia," Flo said.

"So, this is salt?" Ozzy said, gawping.

"One way to find out!" exclaimed Benji as he jumped off his horse, got down on his hands and knees like a dog, and licked the ground. "Yep! It sure is salt!" His eyes were watering as he spoke.

Flo and Ozzy laughed. For the first time, Flo looked into Ozzy's eyes and didn't feel so scared. Ozzy smiled back and blushed a little.

"What's that?" asked Flo, pointing into the distance. A small figure, the size of a cat, seemed to be sat on the salt flat, hovering in the heat. As they drew closer, they could hear a faint crying and to their astonishment, there on the salt, was a small monkey with a black fluffy tail. It was blonde all over, apart from its black eyes, its black scalp, and its black tail. The monkey appeared to be crying. Tears were falling from its little black eyes onto the salty ground. It was clutching its foot.

Flo ran to it. "Oh dear! Are you okay?"

"I have a thorn!" wailed the little monkey. "And I've lost my troop. I'm all alone!" The monkey's tears sizzled on the salt beneath him.

"Oh, poor you! Maybe we can help." Flo called to Flash and asked him for a remedy to help heal the monkey's foot.

Flash and a group of fireflies flew to the scene and looked disapprovingly at the monkey. "We aren't really meant to help the likes of these. They tend to cause a lot of mischief!"

"Oh, please, no! I'm not a bad monkey. I come from the north. Troops from the north are different from the troops from the black mountains!"

Flo picked him up and cuddled him. "We must help him!"

"I'm not sure we should!" said Benji.

"Benji!" Flo cried. "The poor creature needs help!" She was looking to Flash with tears in her eyes.

"As you wish," said Flash. "You have the remedy in your boot pocket. One drop of a tree kiss will heal his wound. He has a thorn in his foot. Squeeze a kiss and the thorn should ease out in no time."

Flo pressed the waxy plant together and a small bead of milky liquid dropped onto the splinter in the monkey's foot. The thorn worked its way out and the creature sighed in relief. Then he wrapped himself around Flo like a woolly scarf and she snuggled him, despite the searing heat.

"What is your name?"

"Boo." The monkey blinked as he spoke.

Although it looked a lot cuter and more lifelike than the shadow monkey he had seen, Benji had a feeling that this monkey was trouble.

On they went, across miles of flat salty ground. Before long, they were beginning to feel tired and thirsty. Flo listened to the fireflies telling her about the wonderful healing benefits of the leaves of the trees while Boo stayed wrapped around her neck. Benji and Ozzy went in front, following Blaze's lead.

"Ewww! What's that?" Flo said.

"What?" asked Benji, darting around with his spear.

"There's something hot and wet trickling down my back."

"Looks like monkey pee," Blaze said.

Benji and Ozzy began laughing so hard they fell to the ground and doubled over. Benji pointed at Flo and tried to speak but the giggles just grew stronger and stronger as they rolled around on the ground.

"It's not funny," Flo said, stroking Boo's little head. His forehead was furrowed. His eyes looked large and penitent. "He must be feeling terrified and your sniggering isn't helping matters."

The boys climbed back onto their horses. Although their laughing had subsided a little, tears still rolled down their cheeks. What Flo had failed to notice was that Boo had a small pointy tube made of bone hidden underneath his hairy armpit. When no one was looking, Boo took what looked like a sharp thorn lodged in his blonde fur like a hairclip. He placed it inside the tube. With one short and rapid blow, he shot the thorn towards Benji's neck faster than an arrow.

"Ouch," said Benji, holding onto his head. But the sting subsided, and he quickly forgot. Soon, however, a shadow seemed to cloud his eyes. Boo stayed curled around Flo's shoulders and pretended to snooze.

Ozzy held his golden dagger in his hand while Benji examined his spear.

"That's a cool dagger you've got there," said Benji. "It's not as powerful as my spear, but I guess I'm taller than you. I suppose it makes sense that I should have the biggest weapon."

"Who says it's better?" Ozzy replied.

"Well, maybe it's not the best. I'm sure they're all useful."

Benji was silent for a moment and then, with a faraway look in his eyes, he said, "You know, it was my Grandpa that first came here. He was the hero then. I'd really like to be the hero now."

Ozzy was silent. He looked sad for a moment. The kind sparkle that Benji saw when they shook hands earlier that day had disappeared. Ozzy's cheeks burned red.

"Have you ever even used a spear?" Ozzy asked. "I bet you don't even know how to throw it!"

"Of course I do!"

Flo interrupted their squabble. "What's going on, you two? I thought you had made up and become friends."

"Friends? Who said we were friends?" Benji said as he squeezed his horse's flanks with his heels and cantered ahead.

17

WISDOM

Before long, the children came across an island covered in tall cacti as far as the eye could see. The silhouette of each cactus looked like a person. Their prickly arms were outstretched to the blazing sun.

"Welcome to the Island of Cacti," Blaze said. "Here we will meet Wisdom. He is the oldest cactus on this island, a thousand years old in fact. He has seen many Fire Children come and go over the centuries, and he is particularly interested in meeting you three."

"Will he know where the children have been taken?" asked Flo.

"I will save them!" said Benji, puffing his chest and flexing his muscles. "We wouldn't be here if I didn't have a battle to win."

Flo looked at him with the same stony stare she always gave when he was being particularly bigheaded. Benji chose to ignore her.

They hiked up a small hill and turned a corner to see an enormous cactus, twenty-feet high, sitting proudly above all the others. He looked across the wide-open saltpans from the highest vantage point of the island while white-winged doves, honeybees and pretty, purple-headed hummingbirds fluttered around him, some perching on his large waxy leaves and spiky arms. The fireflies made merry tunes when they saw the wise old cactus, his leaves and white fruits bursting with magical nectar.

"Welcome, children. I have waited a thousand years to meet you." Wisdom's voice was old and raspy. "The prophecy that you would come to this Island and see me before I die has finally come to pass. You have the power to restore colour and bring hope back to your people."

Then Wisdom squinted in the sun.

"Ah Benji, there you are. You look just like your grandpa."

"Do you know my grandpa?"

"I remember meeting him here when he was just a boy like yourself. And Ozzy, it is an honour to meet you. Once an orphan, but now a Fire Child. A very special reward awaits you."

Ozzy smiled.

"But the battle must go on," Wisdom said. "Prepare your weapons. You must now defeat a great sea monster. He is very close."

Even as he spoke, Benji heard a quiet thudding sound and the ground beneath began to vibrate.

"He is the beast of great division. With his wily wickedness, he can divide kingdoms, families and friends. He is wreaking havoc on earth right now, so make sure you fight together. No hard feelings, now. Otherwise, they will weaken you."

Benji realized he had to say sorry to Ozzy, and quickly. His face began to flush as he tried to swallow his pride, but an angry bubble just kept welling up inside him.

"I'm sorry Ozzy. Your dagger is as great as my spear, probably better! I don't know why I said those mean things to you." Benji tried very hard to feel sorry as well as say it, but it wasn't so easy.

"It's okay. I know I'm special too. The Moon Queen told me. She said I am a Fire Child, just like you!"

"Check your heads for poisonous darts," the great cactus said. "It sounds like you've been caught off guard already."

Blaze flew above each child's head to inspect them. Benji yelped as Blaze pulled out a small grey thorn covered in blood.

Benji rubbed his head. The shadow that had clouded his eyes began to fade and his bright blue sparkle returned.

"What is that?" he said, rubbing his head.

"You have been shot by a dart," Blaze said. "They cause toxic thoughts."

"Be wary of who you let into your circle and always be on guard," Wisdom said. "Make sure there is harmony among you."

Benji looked at Ozzy and nodded and Ozzy nodded back. As they made friends again, their bodies began to glow.

"The sea creature is a wild beast," the cactus said, "and he has divisive power that he uses in both this world and your world. You must pierce his heart and free your people."

It was then that Benji saw it. In the distance, something monstrous was creeping towards them. It was like a crocodile, but no ordinary crocodile.

"That's Leviathon!" Benji shouted. He had been reading about this very beast in his new book from the book fair.

The creature advancing towards them had huge talons. It was three times the size of the sea beast that Benji and Flo had fought in the enchanted cave. Its cylindrical body and fins were slate grey and covered in what looked like metallic fish scales. Most frightening of all, it was breathing black smoke from his mouth. It strode forward, its rippling legs pounding the ground. As smoke bombs shot out of its nostrils, the fireflies hid underneath Wisdom's shade. Boo scuttled behind a big rock.

Benji gripped his tall spear.

"Stand back! I must defeat this beast!"

Flo and Ozzy stepped back. Their hearts were thumping.

As black fire bellowed towards Benji, it looked like each flame had a face that cackled. Benji lifted his shield to stop them burning his skin. He was now surrounded by smoke and flames and he could no longer see the others. His eyes stung and he began to cough as the fumes engulfed him. Then he heard a terrifying voice.

"I can cut you in half with the whip of my tail," the beast said. "But I will spare your life if you let me take you to the Prince. He will give you far more power than the Fire King can. Leave your so-called friends and come with me."

Benji felt dizzy. The smoke was making him feel sick and the more the voice spoke, the weaker he felt.

"Never!" he spluttered, and his body glowed brighter. His spear vibrated with light and power as he sprinted towards the beast's chest. The armour was like a huge scaly wall, so high and wide he could hardly see above and around it. But Benji didn't hesitate. He ran as fast as he could, and he hurled his fiery spear at the centre of the beast's chest. It penetrated the armour and pierced the beast's black heart.

The creature roared like a hundred angry lions. Benji covered his ears and fell to his knees just as the beast crashed to the ground, causing it to crack and open a vast chasm that stretched for miles. Benji almost fell into the crevice but hung onto the edge by his fingertips. He watched the beast and his spear fall deep into the abyss while he hung onto the ledge. When the creature's body had thudded into the ground below, Benji groaned as he tried to heave his tired body up onto the salty ground. Ozzy reached out to grab Benji's hand, pulling him to safety.

"Thanks," gasped Benji. "I've lost my spear."

"I will get it," Ozzy said, as he peered over the edge a hundred feet below. "I will get it somehow." But there didn't seem to be any way down. Just then, a bird flew towards them through the smoky air. It was a huge condor with black wings and a ruff of white feathers around the base of its neck. Its small head was bald, red and featherless.

"Breakfast!" it croaked, looking down into the ravine. "Looks delicious!"

"We need to get down there to get my spear," Benji said.

"Climb on."

The vulture spread its wings like a giant fan. The children mounted the great bird, gripping its feathers with their fingers. Then they dived down into the salty canyon where the giant crocodile lay dead still.

Benji dismounted and pulled his spear out of the beast's chest. Black blood burst out and splattered him in the nose. "Ewww!" he shrieked. Flo and Ozzy screwed their faces up and helped Benji onto the bird, which, after tearing some meat from the beast's carcass and eating its fill, soared again.

The children's faces shone as red as the sunset as they looked down from a great height upon miles of salty ground. As they watched in wonder, the chasm began to close, burying the sea monster.

The children landed among the cacti at the high peak of the hill on the island. They were weary now as they walked to Wisdom, although they felt strengthened by the fireflies singing songs in praise of their victory. A fire was roaring now, and the smell of fire berry tea and baked moon bread made the children's tummies rumble.

Boo jumped on Flo's shoulders and wrapped himself around her neck. Benji collapsed in a heap beside the fire. Boo kept his beady eyes fixed firmly on Benji's spear as the campfire danced and the music played under the giant moon. While the children relaxed, they didn't notice Boo crawling away from Flo.

The monkey crept up behind Ozzy, approaching Benji's spear. His eyes wild with wickedness.

Soon, it would be his.

18

RAINBOW LEAF

As Wisdom told tales of the Shadow Wars, Benji leaned back with his arms folded behind his head and looked up at the bright stars. Then he turned and looked at Flo. She was deep in thought as she looked at the night sky. With her finger, she was joining the stars together in the shape of a key and a door.

The silence was interrupted by Ozzy. "Are we on a different planet?"

"Yes, where exactly are we on the map?" asked Flo.

The wise old cactus smiled. "No map in your world can accurately show the universe because it cannot account for the worlds you cannot always see. But, it might help if you think of a three-dimensional sphere. Earth and Battlelands are intertwined. Earth is what you can see. Battlelands is what you cannot see, not from earth's point of view anyway. Everland is the unseen outer sphere holding all the worlds together."

"That's cool," said Benji, scratching his head.

Benji reached down to grasp his spear.

He leapt into the air and cried, "It's gone!"

Flo jumped. "What do you mean it's gone?"

"My spear. It was here a second ago!"

Blaze flew over and cried, "Boo has stolen Benji's spear! We have just seen him head west, scuttling across the flats in the darkness."

"I knew it!" growled Benji. "I knew he was trouble!"

Flo's face turned grey.

"Next time, we do not trust a monkey!" Benji shouted, staring directly at Flo. She lowered her eyes and clenched her fists. Flo was usually so intuitive with animals, but Boo had bewitched her. Now she felt foolish and wished she had listened to Benji.

"I'm sorry," she said. "His soft cuddles tricked me. It's all my fault." She sat on the salty ground and began to cry.

Wisdom smiled and said, "Don't worry, Flo. Often, after a great victory, the shadows can catch you off guard. Keep your eyes sharp and you will find the spear. But now it's time to sleep. The fireflies will lead the way at sunrise."

"Sleep? Are you mad? I want my spear back!" Benji was looking so exasperated; his cheeks were flushed.

"The Fire King has sent a stillness and we must honour it," Wisdom said. "You can't fight a battle if you haven't rested. Rest is a treasured weapon." His large spikey eyes began to close even as he spoke.

The fireflies started to make tunes as the children curled up like kittens by the fire and fell asleep. They sang,

Arise Fire Child
Resolute and wise
Wield your weapons to the skies
Colour will return
To an ashen world
When the Shadow Prince is defied

Arise Fire Child
Arise, Arise, Arise

As Benji drifted off, he began to dream again. This time, he was standing at the door of Grandma Brook's cottage. He grasped the door handle and pushed. The house was in darkness and he could hear a strange sound coming from the living room.

Benji walked through to the living room to see Grandma Brook snoring in her armchair. To his horror, he saw shadow monkeys darting across the room and climbing the curtains. They knocked a picture of Grandpa Brook onto the floor, as well as the mug of tea that had gone ice cold.

"Get out!" Benji shouted. "Who said you could come in here?" He tried to prod them with his spear, but it passed right through them, as if they were thin air.

The monkeys laughed and made weird screeching sounds as they created chaos. One jumped down and landed on the back of Grandma Brook's armchair and began to clamber all over her head. This made Benji furious. He looked out of the window at the moon lighting up the dark clouds and began to sing the battle song he had just been singing, which was still ringing in his ears.

Arise, Fire Child!
Arise! Arise! Arise!

The monkeys squealed and put their hands over their ears. Then they shot through the window and vanished into the night.

Grandma Brook stirred and opened her eyes. She was startled by the sight of Benji standing by the window. "Benji, is that you? What on earth are you doing here this late at night? Am I dreaming?"

"Yes, it's me, Grandma. I'm not sure if you are dreaming. I think I am, but I couldn't be certain. Maybe we both are. Anyway, I have something important to tell you."

He walked over to Grandma Brook's armchair. "I have been to Battlelands, where Grandpa has been before. Do you remember him telling us?"

"Yes. It was just silly dream."

"It wasn't a dream, Grandma. It was true. I killed Leviathon with my spear and I am going to save the children and bring colour back to our world. You will see! The Shadow Prince has put a curse on all the grownups. He wants everyone to be miserable and believe that everything on earth is dark and hopeless, but it's not true, Grandma. Colours still exist!" Benji's heart felt bigger as he spoke.

"You've lost your marbles, just like your Grandpa!" she croaked.

"No, Grandma," Benji pleaded.

The room filled with moonlight and Grandma Brook looked into her grandson's eyes. As she gazed, she began to soften.

"You remind me of your grandpa," she said, a tear forming in her eye.

Benji held her hand.

"I had a dream once," she said. "A dark hooded figure snatched me from my bed in the middle of the night when I was just a little girl, about your age. He took me to a strange and terrifying land, and trapped me in a big, black tower. And then, your grandpa...oh what a lovely boy he was..."

More tears fell.

"He rescued me! He was my hero. He said I was his fire princess."

Grandma Brook now looked different in the moonlight. Her angry lines faded.

Just then, a dark shadow dashed across the room.

Grandma Brook held onto her left eye and groaned.

"Oh, my head!"

Benji remembered the healing leaf in his boots.

He reached inside his moon boot pocket for the piece of rainbow leaf and a tiny red waxy kiss. Grandma Brook stretched out her bent arm and began to cry.

"Am I dying, Benji?"

"No!"

"Is it time to meet my fire prince again?" She wiped away her tears and looked up at a picture her husband had painted of them under a fire-filled sky. "I remember that day, like it was yesterday. The sunset was so bright the whole sky turned bloodred!"

A light wind blew through the room.

Benji saw an angel shimmering. Her colours were faint, but they were discernible.

"Can you see that?" asked Benji.

The angel's eyes were green and her hair a fiery red. She wore a long pale green dress that flowed like water. Her iridescent wings were wide and filled the room. As Benji stared at her, he saw more angels, less colourful and more transparent, passing in and out of the two worlds.

Grandma Brook's mouth was wide open. "I have never seen anything so beautiful."

The angel smiled and bowed her head as the other angels smiled.

"Just wait until you meet the Moon Queen!" Benji said with a broad grin.

Benji held out the rainbow leaf. He passed the large leaf to his grandmother. She took it and it shimmered in her palm,

"What am I to do with it?"

"Eat it, I suppose."

Grandma Brook laughed. "Well, I've got nothing to lose." With that, she began to nibble on the colourful leaf.

Her tired eyes widened.

"I can taste strawberry, pear, peach, pineapple, cherry and passion fruit!"

Once she had swallowed the whole piece, she began to giggle. "My body is tingling all over!" Soon her giggle turned into a mighty roar of laughter that was so wild she couldn't stop. Benji began to laugh too, and so did all the angels.

"My headache's gone!"

Grandma Brook's head began to glow and the blue in her old grey eyes shone like sapphires. Somehow, she didn't look so old anymore. Her worry lines had vanished, her long-lost smile had returned. Benji had never seen his grandma look so beautiful.

"Now do you believe, Grandma?" Benji gasped.

"I believe!" she cried as happy tears rolled down her coloured cheeks.

Grandma Brook stood up, a bit wobbly at first. She then held onto Benji's hands and began to dance around the room. Benji could not remember seeing his grandma stand up, never mind dance. They laughed so much, Benji's sides hurt.

19

ELIZA

Flo woke up to hear Benji laughing in his sleep beside the red embers of the campfire. It was still dark, and the sun had not yet risen as the fireflies flew over to see what all the commotion was about. Benji laughed and laughed and woke himself up with tears rolling down his face.

"What is it, Benji? What's so funny?"

Benji wiped his eyes. "I had the best dream ever!"

"Tell me!"

"I was in Grandma Brook's cottage and she ate the rainbow leaf and there were angels and she saw them, and we were all laughing and dancing! But..." His happy face turned a little sour. "I guess it was just a dream."

Flick flew in front of Benji's face. "Look in your pocket."

Benji checked his pocket for the rainbow leaf. "It's gone! Does that mean that what I dreamed was real?"

"Remember," Wisdom said, "the seen and the unseen worlds are intertwined. What you dream and imagine can be more real than you realise."

Then his expression changed.

"You must move quickly, across Argus's Bridge. We are not far from his den and he might smell you and have you for breakfast if he wakes up."

The children leapt to their feet, said goodbye to Wisdom, who was now standing with his arms lifted to the sky, and trotted across the flats into some woodland in the far distance. Minutes later, the ground began to tremble and the trees rustle. The sky was now slate grey between the treetops and the rising sun was trapped behind it. The rumbling sound became louder and louder as the horses galloped at full speed, but it was too late. Argus Panoptes was catching up with them. The children needed to prepare for battle more quickly than they had anticipated.

The giant stomped, the earth shook, and the horses bucked in terror. The fireflies scattered, and the children reined in their horses and stood side by side. Benji was powerless without his spear, so he stood with his hands on his hips and his chest extended like a superhero. Flo and Ozzy wielded their weapons, raising them to the sky.

Argus was a many-eyed giant, twenty feet tall, with the body of a gigantic hairy man. His grey head was the size of a huge boulder. Among all the smaller eyes, he boasted one large black eye in the centre of his forehead. There were two silver horns on his head.

The giant held his arms up, his palms facing outwards.

Flo shrieked.

He had an enormous eye set in the palm of each hand.

Flo couldn't look at him. His one big eye in the middle of his forehead was terrifying enough, never mind the other two ogling her from his hands. Then, to add to her horror, she noticed his thick trunk-like legs were also covered in eyes, thousands of them, all leery and staring at her.

Ozzy backed away and hid behind a tree but the branches, like tentacles, curled around his body and tied him to its trunk.

Ozzy screamed.

Flo ran to him and tried to cut him free with her sword, but the tree snatched the sword from her hand and its branches whipped around her body too. It suspended her in the air like an offering.

The giant came close, took Flo from the tree in his big black hairy hand and held her high in the sky. As he swung her round and round in the air like a human mace, she curled up into a tight ball inside his fist. With her eyes squeezed closed, she leaned against his big slimy eyeball and groaned.

Benji looked up at the tree that held Ozzy captive and launched himself at it. He punched the trunk in its eye and shoved his boot in its barky mouth. The tree groaned and let the sword of stones loose. Benji grabbed it, cut Ozzy free and then shimmied up the tree at great speed until he was at the same height as the giant. All the tree climbing and lamppost scaling he had done in the past now paid off as he looked down on the giant.

"Ozzy!" he shouted. Ozzy was making a break for it, but strong weeds twisted up from the ground and lassoed themselves around his ankles. From his feet to his mouth, Ozzy was bound and gagged.

Benji lifted the sword of stones and slashed it across the giant's knuckles. Argus let out an ear-piercing roar and loosened his grip. Flo stood up in the palm of the giant's hand. She grabbed hold of the giant's thumb while Benji hung from his index finger.

Argus roared and then tightened his grasp, squashing Benji and Flo together. Then he bent down and ripped Ozzy out of the grip of the roots. With Benji and Flo in his right hand and Ozzy in his left, he opened his cavernous mouth, ready to hurl them down his reeking and rotten throat. They screamed as they looked at his long, sharp, yellow teeth and his black slimy tongue, flapping around like a gargantuan fish.

Just then, the clouds above them parted and the giant looked up into the sky and grunted. A dazzling white winged horse appeared, with a pretty girl with long black plaited hair riding on the back of it. Her plaits stretched all the way down to her boots. Her ears were long and pointed, her eyes large and brown. She wore a small brown leather tunic and her fur boots held five golden arrows. She had a bow in her hands and, with one sharp shot, she released a golden dart straight towards the head of the giant. Its golden tip pierced the middle eye of his forehead.

Argus growled, spluttered and began to stumble backwards. He buckled and crashed to the earth with an ear-splitting thump. The ground shook so violently that Benji and Flo clung onto each other as they fell in the palm of giant's sweaty hand.

After a brief silence, Benji looked up through a cloud of dust. "Good shot," he said to the girl.

"We must leave quickly," she said. "The giant is only sleeping. My arrows contain a paralysis potion, not powerful enough to kill him."

When Benji stood up, he felt a little faint.

The strange girl took a blade from her bootstrap and cut Ozzy loose.

"Thanks," said Ozzy, rolling out of the palm of the giant's hand and pulling a thick weed from his mouth.

The children followed the girl uphill through the woods until they reached an opening. The view at the top was breath-taking, bursting with colour. A black mountain range stood in the distance, its snowy peaks stretching out like pearls through purple clouds. At the foot of the mountains, a great emerald lake spread out as far as they could see. Rainbow-coloured sand dunes led onto a long beach of pastel stripes.

"What's over there?" asked Flo as she pointed to what looked like a silver path with clusters of tall white trees on either side.

"Glass Woods. We are passing through there now," the girl said as she led them down a steep slope with the tallest trees they had ever seen.

"I'm Benji." Benji's voice was shaky and his cheeks the colour of pomegranates.

"My name is Eliza. I am from the Star Glades to the far east of the realm. Where are you from?"

Benji stared at her, as if in a trance. He didn't seem to hear her question.

"What land are you from?" she asked again.

Benji tried to reply but for some strange reason the words would not come out of his mouth.

Flo had never known him to be so quiet. "We are from earth," she said, "and we are on our way to the Black Mountains to save my little sister Bea, Benji's brother Jo, and our best friend Joanna. The harpies stole them from our world."

"The Black Mountains are perilous. Not many have survived them. Only a Fire Child would succeed."

"I am a Fire Child," Ozzy said. "My name's Ozzy." He flattened his wild black hair with his hands. He was blushing too.

"And I'm Benji and I'm a Fire Child too," Benji interjected, finding his voice again. He walked in front of Ozzy, but Ozzy nudged him to the side.

Flo wondered why they were both acting so strangely.

"We are all Fire Children," insisted Flo.

"If you are not a Fire Child," asked Benji, "then what are you?"

"I am an elf from the Star Glades. We serve the Fire King."

"So do we," said Flo.

"Then we are on the same side. Come with me to the Glades. We have plenty of food and shelter. My village folk will be happy to meet you."

"Thank you," Flo replied.

The fireflies buzzed all around Eliza's head. "And you too, little ones," Eliza said smiling. The fireflies made excited sounds, like windpipes.

"We must pass through Glass Woods, cross Jade Lake and then we should reach the Star Glades by sunset. That's if we don't run into any more trouble."

A few minutes later, the slope was so steep, the children dismounted their horses and slid down on their bottoms.

"This is so cool!" Benji shouted as he landed in a pile of rainbow sand.

Flo combed the colourful sand with her fingers. "I've never seen sand like this before!"

"It's the finest glass-making sand in any of the worlds. You will not find more beautiful vessels made anywhere." Eliza's eyes were glinting like tiger stones as she spoke. "Come this way."

Eliza led the children through the green forest until tall crystal white trees came into view. It was clear for them all to see that the trees were made of glass. You could see rainbow prisms bounce from tree to tree as the sunlight seeped through the treetops above their heads.

"Amazing!" Flo said as she marvelled at the trees reaching out with glass branches, tiny glass birds twittering in their glass nests. "Why is everything made from glass?" Even the path beneath their feet was glass, with beautiful veins of green and blue swirling through it like marble.

"Every time a Fire Child suffers a blow, the glass blowers blow," Eliza answered.

None of them knew what she meant.

But it wouldn't be long before they found out.

20
THE GLASS BLOWERS

Flo felt as if she was in a dream as a huge dome-shaped house appeared at the end of the winding path. It had many windows, each one glowing with amber. At each one, she could see the silhouette of a little person blowing through a long pipe. The glass house sparkled in every colour imaginable.

Eliza led the children to the main entrance, which was wide open. They stood in a great glass hallway shaped like a wavy dome. Colourful glass pictures hung on the walls. Glass objects were suspended in glass cabinets. Lions and angels and other glass sculptures were dotted everywhere amongst tall vases of rainbow sand. Glass moons, stars and hearts were hanging from the ceiling. A golden glass pitcher, along with drinking glasses, was laid out on a blue glass table.

As Flo gazed at the table, a short and wide-eyed lady shuffled through a doorway. She had a rotund face and peachy curled hair. "Hello little ones, my name is Rose Gold. What a joy to see you. Would you like a drink?" She began to pour water from the golden glass pitcher before the children had time to answer.

"Thank you," Flo said, feeling quite overcome and a little amused that the diminutive lady was calling them 'little ones', as she was half their height.

"There's so much glass!" Benji exclaimed, whizzing around the room and almost knocking over a large lion. It wobbled and then fell back into place.

"There's no escaping the fiery trials," Rose Gold muttered. "Would you like to see yours?"

The children stared at each other, a confused look on their faces.

Then they nodded.

The lady led them down a glass tubular corridor and into a round, glowing room where hundreds of kilns were burning. Ruddy-faced little men and women stood beside each kiln, shaping red blobs of molten glass at the end of their blowing pipes.

"I would like to congratulate you on your most recent victory. Killing the croc is no easy feat," the lady said.

"Here's the end result," said a sweaty little man sitting on a stool and sipping a glass of water. He pointed proudly to a glass sculpture of a boy that looked remarkably like Benji, slaying a beastly crocodile. The children marvelled at the detail. Benji's spear even had a flaming tip.

"We don't always sculpt the exact representation of the trial you go through. Often, we make a jewel, a prize or a trophy, but this was such a spectacle, it just had to be done!" The little man was beaming as he spoke.

"Come," said the little lady. "I will show you where we store the treasure."

Ozzy and Flo followed while Benji continued to stare at the sculpture of himself. "Thanks," Benji said to the glass blower.

"Oh no, thank you, Benji Brook. You killed the croc!" The man lifted his tiny arms high in triumph. He laughed so much he almost fell off his stool.

Rose Gold led the children down a corridor with many rooms, where little people were moulding and crafting fine jewels and metals with blowtorches and sharp blades. Then they followed her up a set of glass stairs that spiralled to another floor with big, bronze, round doors. Rose Gold looked at Flo and motioned to a round rose-tinted glass plaque. Flo Knightly's name was written in gold.

The lady opened the door. The children gasped. The room was full of treasure. Glass birds in many different colours and all shapes and sizes hung from the ceiling, along with a collection of mini beasts made of silver and diamond.

In the centre of the chamber stood an ornate dressing table and, on it, Flo could see the finest and most precious jewellery - strings of pearls in baby pink and duck-egg blue, a gold pendant, a silver and rose-gold bracelet in a Celtic twist and a large ruby ring. But what caught Flo's eye was a brooch made of sapphire, embossed with silver and tiny pink diamonds, set in the shape of her initials: FK.

As Flo continued to marvel at the jewellery, Benji and Ozzy wandered up the corridor looking for their own chambers of treasure. Ozzy opened the door with his name on it, but he didn't expect to see much. He had decided that there would not be much treasure for him because he had caused trouble for most of his life.

He tried to open the door, but there was something obstructing it. He took a deep breath and heaved it open with all his might. The round room was crammed full of treasure. There was so much gold it hurt his eyes. Treasure chests were piled high. And on the glass shelves that covered every inch of the walls right up to the ceiling, there was a golden crown, embossed with rubies and diamonds, a diamond sword and a golden trophy with his initials and his date of birth.

Ozzy scratched his head and wondered if he had entered the wrong room, but then he noticed that the crown had his name embossed into the gold.

Benji ran out of his room into the corridor with a golden medallion hanging from his neck. He held a gold sceptre in his right hand, with the head of a golden lion.

"Look what I've got, Ozzy! Do you think we can keep them?"

"Not right away," Rose Gold replied. "All your treasure is to be transported to the City of Rainbows. You will receive it at your appointed time. There are bigger trials ahead, but do not lose heart! When you suffer a blow, the glassblowers blow!"

"Is this really mine?" asked Ozzy.

"Absolutely, little one!"

"But I haven't done anything to deserve it." Ozzy was downcast.

"Oh, the treasure isn't forged for you because of what you've done but because of who you are. You are a Fire Child. The more you have been through the fire, the more treasure is produced."

Ozzy looked at the golden crown on the glass shelf. *What fire?* he wondered, scratching his head and feeling a deep urge to try it on.

"Those special crowns are made for the children that have never known what it is like to be in a real family. They're for the ones that have never belonged. Go on. Put it on."

Ozzy felt rather silly and for a minute, he wondered what everyone would think. But then he placed the crown on top of his head, and it fitted perfectly. A rush of energy rippled through his body, like an electrical current.

Ozzy looked stunned, but then he felt heat in his head and a deep sense of importance filled his mind. His eye caught sight of a large golden mirror, the full length of the room, resting against the wall. He looked at himself, lifted his head high and straightened his posture. He looked like a true prince, and with that thought, he knew that all this treasure really did belong to him.

As Ozzy continued to look, he saw the faint outline of the fire man he had met in his dream standing beside him, his eyes burning bright, his face smiling.

Ozzy smiled back.

"There you go," Rose Gold said.

Ozzy turned to her and smiled, then he looked back, but the man was gone and Flo and Benji were stood in his place, holding their treasures.

"You can keep your treasure in good time," she said as she placed Ozzy's crown back on the glass shelf and retrieved Benji's golden medallion and Flo's brooch.

She paused, looked at the children, and then spoke.

"It's time to find your brothers and sisters. No doubt more treasure will be made along the way."

21

THE STAR GLADES

The children left the glass dome and headed towards a green lake where a large wooden boat was tied to a jetty. The vessel was just big enough to allow three horses and three children on board. The fireflies, Eliza and her white-winged horse flew in the sky above them. Ozzy and Flo took an oar each and rowed west at Eliza's request.

The journey took several hours, but the children were never bored as shoals of mermaids with rainbow tails swam beneath them. Benji dived into the emerald lake and grinned underwater with his long, white hair flowing above him as the mermaids swam around him, surfacing from time to time to wave at the others.

Luminous butterflies danced together, making mesmerising shapes, as the children reached a sandy beach and disembarked. The butterflies morphed into the shape of an arrow and shot through a small wood. The children followed.

Tiny balls of colourful light hovered above an enormous clearing. The children gawped to see hundreds of elfin people like Eliza lying down on the ground and peering through telescopes at a circular opening in the treetops. Their eyes were shaped like almonds. Besides the stargazers, there were many others trading goods in a marketplace filled with colourful yurts and tents. Campfires blazed as cooking pots sizzled. Some sat around merrily drinking from what looked like coconut shells.

Delicious smells filled the air and the children's tummies rumbled as they saw tables outside stalls covered in delicious delicacies. Stringed instruments sounded and elfin children laughed as they played games between the trees that lined the village. When they saw Benji, Ozzy and Flo, they stopped hiding and gathered, whispering excitedly.

Some of the elves sat shining their boots and swords. Others sharpened their arrows and fixed their bows. Benji marvelled at the outline of angels joining in and talking with the elves, nodding and smiling. When the angels saw the children, they stopped and knelt before them, tilting their heads to the ground.

"Welcome to Lazuli of the Star Glades," said a tall angel. As she drew closer, her appearance became more solid. "I am Humility." She bowed low and, as she did, her long silver hair and dress moved like liquid. Her whole body looked like it was made of water as she shone in faint blues and greys. Her eyes were fiery amber, and her face was exquisite. Benji, Flo and Ozzy didn't say a word. They simply bowed back.

"Do not bow. I am your servant, simply a creature of light, and I am honoured to meet you." She bowed low again.

The children stood up straight, feeling a little silly.

"Why are the elves looking at the stars?" Flo asked.

"The elves have been star gazing for centuries. Did you know that the Fire King's plan to flood the earth with colour again is written in the stars?"

"Wow!" Benji cried as he gazed up into the sky and caught a glimpse of the outline of all three of them.

"You must be thirsty," she said.

Three young elves walked over, carrying coconut shells filled with milk and fire berries. The children drank the sweet liquid. The fire berries warmed their bellies and made them tingle.

"This is a cool place," Benji said, his lips all milky.

Ozzy nodded. "Yeah, it's not what I expected."

"What did you expect?" the angel asked.

"I guess I thought we would be fighting dark beasts all the time."

"Like in your world?"

"No, there are no dark beasts there."

"None that you can see," Humility said.

"I guess not. Ours is a gloomy world, all black and white. Nothing like here."

"We know our King," Humility said. "And we hope that the war will be over soon. Come, you must be hungry."

"Starving!" Benji said.

Eliza led the children under a purple, triangular canopy to a long table containing a myriad of delicacies. The fruits, leaves, berries, cakes, moon muffins, pies and puddings made the air smell sweet. In the centre, there was a fountain of dark, bubbling chocolate topped with flecks of gold.

"Help yourself," said an elf.

They each took a plate and piled it high with as much food as they could. Not long after they had filled their tummies, they felt a little dreamy as they finished off their hot sparkly chocolate from small round wooden bowls. They reclined on velvet cushions and fell fast asleep.

Once again, Benji began to dream.

He was clinging to the edge of a jagged cliff high up in the mountain. He watched as his spear fell thousands of feet below. He felt weak and powerless. Then a great beast, even bigger that the monstrous crocodile Benji had defeated, pounded over to where he was hanging. The beast looked like a buffalo, a rhinoceros and a man, all morphed together. Benji knew he was going to die, but just as the beast was about to step on Benji's fingers, a blinding light blazed, and the beast fell back.

In the great light stood the outline of a tall, strong man. His body was on fire and his eyes were aflame. Benji climbed up and knelt before him, squinting in the radiant light, watching as the man's face kept changing from the face of a boy, to a man, to a warrior to a lion and then to an eagle and then back to a man again. He lifted the huge beast with one hand and tossed it over the edge of the cliff to its death.

The fire man reached out, grabbed hold of Benji's hand and helped him up onto his feet. Benji struggled to look him in the eyes. Then a great voice roared like a thousand lions. "My fire will make you strong."

Benji clutched his burning chest as pearls of sweat rolled down his face. He breathed heavily and whimpered.

"Wake up, Benji!" Flo cried, shaking him. "You're dreaming again!"

Benji opened his eyes. "I saw a man, a terrifying man. He was so bright I couldn't look at him!"

"Was it the Shadow Prince?" Ozzy asked.

"No, he was wonderful, but terrifying and strong and bright, like fire!"

"That's the Fire King," Ozzy said, remembering the wonderful presence of the man he met in his dream.

The fireflies flew over to tend to Benji's distress. Flick wiped his brow with a large minty blue leaf. When Flick noticed the small thorn lodged in the back of Benji's head, she removed it.

"Ouch!"

"No wonder you have been having nightmares. It looks like that meddling monkey shot you with another toxic dart. Remember those nasty little thorns can darken thoughts and dreams." She put some cooling ointment on the back of his head where the dart had pierced him. Benji began to calm down.

"There, you will start to think more clearly now."

"I think it was the Fire King," Benji said. "He's much more powerful than anyone else, but when I looked at him I felt like I was going to die. My spear fell down the mountain and I was hanging onto the cliff edge. There was a huge buffalo-like monster, and he was going to push me off, but then the Fire King saved me."

Blaze and all the fireflies chuckled. "Yes," Blaze said. "He has that effect. And he has a way of turning our bad dreams into good ones. Now, don't you worry. He has picked you out for a reason, Benji. What did he say?"

"That his fire will make me strong. When he said that, I felt a burning in my heart."

At that moment, Humility arrived. "The beast in your dream is Behomoth," she said. "He's the biggest beast of all and tries to trick you into thinking that without your weapon you are powerless, but the Fire King is telling you that even without your spear, his fire will make you strong."

Benji nodded, his heart still burning.

22
LOG CABIN

Blaze looked at the children with a forlorn expression. "We can take you as far as the meadows," she said, "but then, you must go the rest of the journey alone."

"Alone!" Flo exclaimed. "Why aren't you coming with us?"

"Fireflies cannot survive the high altitude of the mountains, but we have drawn you a map and we have packed you some food for the journey. You have shown you are very capable of surviving. You don't really need us anymore."

Flo cupped Blaze in her hands and began to cry. "You have been such a helpful little guide and I will miss you so much!"

Blaze glowed warmly in her palms. Flo wished she could keep Blaze in her pocket and take him back to earth. She wondered if she would ever see the fireflies again.

The children mounted their horses and the fireflies lit the way through the trees that encircled Lazuli village. Then they said goodbye to the children, who cantered across the meadow while the sun began to rise. Higher and higher it rose, the higher and higher they climbed up the hill. In time, the slopes became steeper and darker, causing the horses to slip on the rocks.

"Look ahead," Ozzy cried, lifting his eyes from a map. "There's a symbol of a blue pool and a pink bird." It wasn't long before the ground levelled out and they came across a sapphire lagoon at the foot of a snow-capped mountain. Raindrops were falling gently from the silver sky and splashing on the steamy, still water that stretched out before them. Hundreds of pink flamingos paddled in the shallows.

"Come and bathe!" a flamingo called out as it walked over to them on rainbow legs shrouded in steam.

The children marvelled at the flamingos dipping and lifting their legs in the lagoon like pink ballerinas. They dismounted their horses and headed over to them.

"It's lovely in here," said another flamingo as the children bent down to test the water. When they felt how warm it was, they stripped down to their vests and waded into the pool. As they began to tread water, their bodies tingled as if sinking into a hot bath.

"This feels like heaven!" said Benji.

Flo smiled. All her worries seemed to evaporate with the warm steam. "Flash said that the sulphur in these waters helps us live longer," she said. With one leg standing straight, and one leg bent, she pointed her toes out of the water just as the flamingos were doing. Meanwhile, Benji and Ozzy lay back in the water with their heads facing the mountain summit. They smiled sleepily and for a few fleeting moments forgot all about the battle that lay ahead.

Just then, Flo had a thought. "Wait a minute. It's just occurred to me that although sulphur is a naturally occurring mineral, it is found in hot springs and volcanic craters."

The boys opened their eyes wide and stared up at the black mountain.

"So, this mountain is a volcano?" Ozzy asked.

"Yes."

As they gawped at the mountain, they saw a group of dark creatures flying in the very far distance.

Ozzy was the first to react. "I don't know what they are, but I suggest we get dressed. Quickly!"

The children put their clothes on at double speed and climbed onto their horses,

"Thank you!" Flo shouted to the unflustered flamingos. They didn't seem to have a care in the world. They stared back, curtseyed, and then bowed their pink heads.

As the dark creatures flew ever closer, the children managed to hide amongst a cluster of trees.

"Harpies!" Benji whispered.

"At least it means we are headed in the right direction," Ozzy said. He unrolled the map. "The harpies are flying from the summit of the mountain, not far from the Shadow Prince's fortress."

"That is where we will find the children and…" Just as Flo was about to finish her sentence, the branch of a tree hit her hard over the head. It caused her to spin towards its trunk and then lodged in her mouth, gagging her.

"Flo!" Ozzy shouted. "Get off her, you dingbat!"

Ozzy cut her loose with his dagger and chiselled out the branch that had stuffed itself in her mouth.

"Thanks," Flo said, looking Ozzy in the eyes again. It was then that she noticed for the first time that he was quite handsome. She felt her cheeks turn pink.

As they regrouped, the children could see the angry faces of the trees. They were not on the Fire King's side and they were not going to let them get away without a fight. As the branches lashed out, they whipped and twisted the children around, tripping them up and coiling them into the tight grip of their trunks. Flo and Ozzy responded by using their sword and dagger. They managed to cut them all loose. They ran towards their horses, but just as they were about to ride away, the harpies encircled the air above them, cackling, shrieking and squawking.

"Come with us and we will free the others," one harpy said. Its voice was sickening.

"Never!" Benji shouted.

A black-haired harpy stretched out her long claws towards Ozzy. "Ha, ha! The little orphan is coming with us!"

"No!" Flo cried.

But it was too late. In one swoop, the harpy snatched Ozzy with her sharp claws and lifted him. Ozzy tried to drop the map for Flo and Benji, but another harpy seized it and ripped it into tiny pieces. They laughed so wildly at this that Flo had to cover her ears as the paper fragments fell like snow to the ground.

The harpies carried Ozzy high into the sky and away towards the summit of the mountain.

"No!" Flo cried, tears streaming down her face. "This wasn't in the plan! We were meant to stay together!"

Benji picked up a large stone and tried to hurl it at the harpy carrying Ozzy away into the sky, but it was no use. He kicked the ground and punched the air. "If I'd had my spear, I could have stopped them!"

Benji and Flo trekked for hours without saying a word. "It doesn't feel the same without Ozzy," Benji said at last.

Flo's eyes welled with tears. "He is a brave and sweet boy," she said as the tears spilled over.

The sky soon became dark and moonless and the climb became steeper. The children began to realize that the horses would not be able to make it to the summit. Flo kissed her horse's soft flat nose and patted her neck. She hooved the ground and looked deep into Flo's eyes.

"She's warning us to be careful," Flo said. "She senses danger ahead."

The horses turned back and descended the jagged slopes, their white manes glowing in the dark as they turned back to Lazuli village.

As the children ascended, the slopes became steeper and icier.

"I wish we had an ice pick," Benji said as they stopped for breath every few yards.

The sky was now pitch black and their only light was from the sword of stones that Flo held in front of them.

Just when they were at their most weary, they caught sight of a glowing light in the distance. As they drew closer, they saw what looked like a log cabin with candles glowing in the window. Smoke billowed from its chimney and the smell of burning wood filled the air.

Both children gave a sigh of relief.

"Shelter," Benji cried.

23

PYTH

Flo knocked on the door as Benji peered inside the cabin. There was a fire burning brightly in a hearth with comfy chairs surrounding it. A cooking pot was bubbling on a stove, minded by a tall man in a pale green velvet cloak. His long straight hair was slick and rainbow-coloured.

The tall man bent over the stove stirring the pot several times, then turned to look at them with startled eyes, as purple as amethyst. "Come in," he grinned, his eyes shining. "You must be Benji and Flo. I've been expecting you."

The warmth from the cabin was like a dream come true. Benji and Flo felt desperate to sit down and rest.

"Epiphany has told me all about you," he said. The man was so tall, he walked with his head ducked beneath the wooden beams of the cabin ceiling. "I'm making a warm stew for you. It gets chillier the higher you climb, doesn't it? And I have baked some delicious cookies." He gave Benji a knowing smile and his teeth shone like the moon. "Come and sit by the fire. You must be exhausted."

As he smiled at them, his gaze seemed hypnotic.

The children shuffled over to two furry armchairs and sat down.

It was like sinking into a cloud as the soft fleece touched their aching bodies. As their tummies rumbled, the heat from the fire warmed their bones.

"What is your name?" Benji asked.

"Pyth." His skin glowed with a faint lilac hue as he spoke.

Flo snatched a furtive glance at Pyth's eyes and then looked down again at the floor. She had a bad feeling in the pit of her stomach. Pyth's eyes were like dark tunnels of strange fire, but not the fire she had seen in the Moon Queen's eyes. She stared at Benji, but he was entranced by the man.

"I'm the Moon Queen's brother," Pyth said, his skin seemed to shimmer in faint scales of pale blue and violet.

"Pleased to meet you." Benji's reply sounded almost robotic.

"Who is Epiphany?" Flo asked, still staring at the floor.

"Why, the Moon Queen of course," said Pyth.

The man's magnetic presence was intensifying.

"Here! Drink some hot cocoa," he said, passing them both a blue wooden bowl with sweet dark liquid in it. "It's made with the finest tree milk."

Benji drank.

"Mmm, it's delicious!"

Flo smelt the drink. She remembered what Flash had taught her about tree milk and how you must be careful, because if it's taken from a cursed tree, it contains dark power.

Flo took a small sip and straightaway she felt a little weaker, as though her heart was incapable of resisting the pull towards the enchanting man. She stopped drinking and stayed very quiet. Flo was not going to be tricked again, she was certain of that. So, she pretended to drink the milk as the man glided across to the stove and served some stew. He placed two bowls painted with moons and stars on a tray with a glass of rainbow milk and a delicious looking cookie.

"Here you are," he said, placing the tray of food on a small table by their side.

"Thank you. It smells yum!" Benji said, as Pyth returned to the stove.

Flo tried to make eye contact with Benji to warn him not to eat, but it was too late. He had drunk all the cocoa and he was already tucking into the food and enjoying every mouthful.

"Benji," Flo whispered.

Benji was in a trance.

"Benji!" she whispered. "I don't trust him."

Benji looked up and said, "Ah, he's okay. He's the Moon Queen's brother."

Flo could see from his docile look that the dark power in the drink was making him woozy.

Flo pursed her lips. "I'm sorry," she said to Pyth. "I'm not feeling very hungry. I'm feeling a little sick."

"Oh dear, those wicked monkeys must have shot you. They're nothing but trouble. Let me give you something to remedy that."

Pyth's eyes flashed like purple flames. There was no doubt in Flo's mind that this man was trouble. Benji, on the other hand, was completely enamoured by his psychedelic charm and the delicious freshly baked cookie he was devouring, which tasted out of this world. It was filled with golden fudge pieces, silvery balls of caramel and dark chocolate chips that melted in his mouth. He grinned sleepily as the chocolate sauce that smothered his top lip turned into a moustache.

Pyth glided to the corner of the room where a large wooden chest was set into a cove in the wall. Above it, a lantern burned. Pyth opened the lid of the chest.

"I have the perfect remedy for your symptoms. It might make you a little sleepy, but the rest will do you good."

Flo looked at Benji. Her eyes narrowed as she tried to indicate with her face that this man was trouble. Benji finished swallowing the last bit of cookie and shook his head as if to say he didn't understand.

Just as Flo was motioning with her hands that they need to run away, Benji spotted Boo the monkey moving in and out of the bottom of the man's cloak.

He dropped his glass of milk in shock. "Oops! Sorry," he said in a slurred voice. He tried to stand up, but his legs wouldn't move. His whole body was beginning to feel very achy and stiff. He tried to speak but his tongue wouldn't cooperate. It swelled and stiffened inside his mouth as his vision became misty. The next moment, he was snoring in a deep and uncontrollable sleep.

Flo gulped as she looked out of the window at the moonless sky. All she could think to do was sing, but it felt so ridiculous. How would singing to the Fire King possibly help? But as Benji snored and dribbled like an old man in his huge armchair, she had to do something.

"Here you go," Pyth said as he handed Flo a silver goblet encrusted with tiny purple stones. Inside there was dark green water with ruby-red flowers floating in it. Flo knew exactly what this was as Flash had warned her.

"Never, under any circumstances, eat red flowers from dead wood mixed with the waters of Jade Lake. It will turn you black and white and overwhelm you with your deepest fears."

The thought of losing colour again was too much to bear. She took the glass from the man who continued to grin, his purple eyes watching Flo's every move.

Flo looked at the horrible green water and tried to stall.

"So, the Moon Queen is your sister. Are you a king, then?"

The man looked at her, unable to disguise his irritation.

"No."

"Why not?"
"I am a warlock."

24

CHESS

Pyth smiled at Flo, his white teeth glowing in the half light. "I believe we have a little friend in common," he said.

The warlock patted his cloak and Boo crawled out from under him, while a pale yellow python curled its way up Pyth's body, wrapping itself around his shoulders.

Flo could feel the pulse in her throat throbbing as her hand gripped the goblet of green water. Although she was scared, she also felt furious. She cleared her throat and began to hum the battle song she had learned.

Pyth's face began to contort.

"Stop that!" he cried as the purple in his eyes turned as black as the night. Flo found the courage to look at them. They flickered like black flames. As she stared at them, she carried on singing, this time louder, and with more confidence.

Arise Fire Child
Resolute and wise
Wield your weapons to the skies
Colour will return

To an ashen world
When the Shadow Prince is defied

Arise Fire Child
Arise, Arise, Arise

The bluish glow that shone from Pyth's skin grew darker and darker until his whole body was slate grey scales. He no longer looked like a man. He looked like a man-snake. His face was shimmering in purples and blue and becoming more triangular shaped, and his eyes and mouth seemed to shrink back into his head.

As Flo continued to sing, she was filled with that same wonderful light she had felt when she had fought the snake-beast. Her body glowed like the moon and her eyes shone like the sun. Pyth staggered forward to grab her, but an invisible wall blocked his way. He clawed at it like a wild animal, growling as he flailed her arms. All the while, Flo carried on singing, the little hairs on her skin standing up as her melody filled the room.

Grimacing in pain, Pyth whispered to the small yellow and white python, his lips touching its scaly skin. It nodded and then slithered underneath the chair where Benji was fast asleep.

Flo dropped her goblet, stood up and held on tightly to the sword of stones. The python slithered up the back of Benji's armchair and into his mop of blonde hair. She stepped towards Benji, whose head and neck were now smothered by the constricting coils of the snake's slimy body. When she saw its head begin to slide into his mouth, she screamed. "No!"

Flo lurched forward, grabbed its throat and pulled it, but as she yanked at it, the serpent tightened its grip around Benji's neck. His face began to turn red, his mouth started to splutter.

Flo's eyes burned with the flames of the Fire King as she throttled the snake with all her might. The snake slowly began to yield.

"I have defeated a bigger snake than you!" she shouted as she pulled the uncoiling reptile away from Benji, who was now coughing and turning back to his normal colour.

Benji's blue eyes opened wide as he saw Flo jumping around the room, fighting the yellow snake she was trying to kill. It writhed around in the air as she whipped it up and down, against the walls and the ground. Flo continued to sing, and as soon as Benji started to join her, their power increased.

Arise Fire Child
Resolute and wise
Wield your weapons to the skies

Colour will return
To an ashen world
When the Shadow Prince is defied

Arise Fire Child
Arise, Arise, Arise

As their song ended, Flo snapped the snake's neck with her bare hands. She twisted it until it was dead and then she hurled it into the fire. The embers hissed and crackled and then burst into flames.

Flo and Benji turned to look at Pyth standing behind the invisible wall. Boo was wrapped around his shoulders, sniggering. Pyth was smirking at them, as if he knew something they didn't.

Flo and Benji started to sing again while more baby pythons appeared, accompanied by an army of scorpions scuttling into the chamber from underneath the armchairs. Benji stomped on the snakes while Flo cut off their heads with her sword. Then they trampled on the scorpions, hearing their pincers crack under their boots.

At that moment, Rainbow fluttered into the room and flew in front of Benji and Flo. The log cabin was filled with a brilliant light. Hundreds of butterflies danced around the room and, as they did, the Moon Queen appeared.

"Well done, you two!" As she spoke, the room seemed to be alive with the faint and wonderful presence of angels who cheered and bowed towards Benji and Flo.

The Moon Queen smiled and then turned to Pyth and Boo, who were quivering in the corner of the room.

"Pyth," the Moon Queen shouted. "How dare you try to poison the Fire Children? When will you give up? Is it still not clear to you that you will never win a battle against a Fire Child?"

Pyth sneered and Boo bared his sharp grey teeth, shaking his head, uttering an ugly snigger.

"Every war you wage only makes them stronger," the Moon Queen said.

As she spoke, Benji saw his spear glowing on a shelf above the fire. He walked over and picked it up. "I believe this belongs to me!" he said, staring at Boo.

Boo quaked and Pyth slumped down to the ground. It looked as if he was weakening with every word the Moon Queen spoke.

The Moon Queen looked at Pyth. "I forbid you to provoke Benji and Flo again. Now go!"

As the Moon Queen shouted the last word, a blinding ball of white fire shot out of her mouth and engulfed Pyth and Boo.

Pyth shrieked, "No!" He writhed around on the ground and morphed into a huge black python with white stripes. He wrapped his scaly body around Boo and they vanished.

The Moon Queen turned to Benji and Flo. "Keep singing and you will regain your strength. You are not far from the children whom you seek."

Then she was gone, while the angels lingered. One angel stoked the fire, while others tidied the room, removing the dead snakes and the scorpions.

Benji sat down on the blanket laid out in front of the fire. There were moon muffins, fire berry tea and a chessboard at his feet.

"You can't still be hungry," Flo said.

"Always hungry." Benji rubbed his belly as he took a big bite out of a muffin.

Flo turned her attention to the game. This was no ordinary chessboard. Instead of the squares being black and white, they were silver and gold. Each chess piece was made of glass and shone with every colour of the rainbow.

Flo played Benji and won. She always won and this usually made Benji super cross, but he was so exhausted he convinced himself it was because he was so tired, and that he would beat her in the morning.

As the tall angels stood guard and the firewood crackled, Benji and Flo soon fell into a deep sleep.

25

THE SUMMIT

Bright rays from the sun blazed through the windows of the log cabin as Benji and Flo woke up from a long, deep sleep. They stretched like cats and tried to move from their armchairs, but their bodies ached. They both wondered how they would manage another day climbing the steep slopes to the summit. The angels were nowhere to be seen, but their presence remained, and it was becoming clear to Benji and Flo that they were in fact never alone; the angels were always there, just invisible.

Flo reached into the pocket of her moon boot and pulled out a spiky leaf with purple berries. "Here," Flo said, passing a berry to Benji. "Flash said they are full of energy. Hopefully they will wake us up a little."

They both popped the purple berry into their mouth and immediately their eyes lit up. As they chewed the fruit, a warm liquid oozed out. It tasted like nothing they had ever eaten before. It was like a hot blueberry with a strong minty taste that made their noses burn a little and their eyes water. The tingling sensation that started in their heads seemed to permeate their bodies, filling them with a surge of energy.

They jumped to their feet and left the log cabin, eating their leftover moon muffins on the way. Benji's spear and Flo's sword became useful walking sticks as they sunk their moon boots into the thick cold snow. The sky was electric blue and not a cloud was in sight as they climbed further and further up the mountain.

They stopped to rest every twenty minutes or so to catch their breath and eat another energy berry.

"Do you think anyone will believe us when we get back to earth?" Benji asked.

"I don't know," Flo replied as they sat looking out at the breath-taking view of Battlelands. Flo was about to continue when the ground began to tremble. "Did you feel that?"

"Yes," Benji said, placing his hand on the rocks. "You did say this is a volcano, didn't you?"

The ground began to tremor a little stronger this time. The children held onto each other. Looking up, they saw an avalanche of snow falling towards them.

"Run!" Benji shouted as he held onto Flo's hand. They went as fast as they could, missing the flood of snow by inches.

The higher they climbed, the steeper it became, until they could not even crawl because the rockface was now vertical. They leaned back on a black boulder with bewildered expressions, wondering how they were going to reach the top without ropes.

Benji had received climbing lessons in his own world and he knew very well how to climb with ropes and clip on to the rock at certain points to avoid a dangerous fall. But they were not well equipped.

"Perhaps we should ask the Fire King," Flo said.

"How do we do that?"

"Sing, I guess."

The children closed their eyes and hummed the tune of the battle song. As they continued, the face of the Fire King filled their minds.

At once, a strong wind blew, cooling their sweaty bodies. Then, from out of nowhere, a familiar orb of light started to shine before them.

"Is that Cast!?" they cried.

Cast appeared with his wide feathered wings. He towered above them, his golden fiery locks flowing and glowing, just like they had in Witch Wood. His eyes swirled in fiery amber as he walked towards them, making huge footprints with his bronze bare feet in the crunchy snow.

Cast held onto the children's hands and they flew up above the steep rockface. He then bowed low before them and said, "You are very close to the summit of the volcano where a dangerous battle is taking place. Angels are fighting dark shadows as we speak. The Shadow Prince intends to sacrifice a child held captive in the black tower."

"No!" Flo cried.

"Why?" asked Benji.

"It is a ritualistic killing, in order to please the Shadow Prince. Every year when he sacrifices a child, his dark powers increase. And the more his darkness fills the world, the more the colour drains away." Cast stood up straight, his wide wings filling their vision. "You must rescue them."

As Cast flew high into the sky, Benji and Flo looked at each other, feeling helpless. The sky darkened and stripes of bloodred streaked through the clouds. Harpies began to appear, and Cast threw balls of lighting fire towards them. A myriad of fiery angels joined forces as the shadowy creatures scattered across the sky.

Terror gripped Flo as she sat in the snow with her fists clenched. But as her tears fell onto the snow, blue flowers, like the forget-me-nots that grew in her garden at home, sprung up from the earth. She smiled as she watched them bloom before her eyes. "Look, Benji," she said as she knelt and pointed at them.

Benji gripped his spear and Flo held onto her sword. Their weapons began to vibrate, and a faint musical sound came from them, as if the weapons had begun to sing the battle song. Benji and Flo continued to climb and sing until they were almost at the top. Then, the faint sound of drums and horrible shrieking began to fill the air. Their hearts pounded as they hopped between geyser holes in the ground. From time to time, these perforations spewed steaming water into the air.

"Hide behind here," Benji said, leading Flo to a huge boulder. From their hiding place, they watched as hundreds of dark shadows and beasts of all kinds stood in a circle around the mouth of the volcano where a lake of fire spat out sparks of crimson lava. They moved on from the rock and crawled to what looked like a watchtower made of black glass. But as they approached it, they saw that there were no entrances or windows. Yet, through the thick dark glass, they could see the outline of many children. Their faces looked haunted and pale as they pressed their hands against the glass.

"How do we get in?" Benji asked. He had tried to crack open the dark glass but to no avail.

Flo waved at the children, but they couldn't see her as she pressed her face against the transparent wall.

"Jo! Bea! Joanna!"

"Do you see them?"

"Yes!" Flo cried, thudding the glass with her fist.

Flo waved, but the children still could not see her. "We will save you," she whispered with tears in her eyes.

As she wiped her cheeks, she spotted a familiar face. "Ozzy!" she exclaimed. She could see him holding a group of little children that had huddled up to him.

Benji knocked on the glass again, but no one could hear them.

"There are so many of them!" Flo cried.

"We must rescue them all," Benji said.

26

THE SACRIFICE

Ozzy stroked the heads of the little children locked inside the damp and shadowy tower. "Don't worry," he said. "The Moon Queen will rescue us."

"Tell us about the Moon Queen again!" pleaded a pretty girl with dark brown eyes and brown skin. Others joined in too. "Please, please!" they cried. There were many different accents. Some spoke in different languages.

Ozzy told them about the Fire King and that they were all Fire Children.

"The Fire King is far more powerful than the Shadow Prince and one day the evil prince will be gone forever!" The children hung on every word.

"Let me see your dagger, Ozzy! Please, please!" said a little boy.

"One day, you will be a warrior and slay a dragon," Ozzy said as the little boy touched the bronze handle of his dagger and marvelled at the sharp curve of the golden blade.

Ozzy smiled at them as he leant back against the dark glass wall with his dagger in his hand. Then he let out a big sigh; he had scaled every inch of the wall but failed to work out an escape route.

The little children sang the battle song that Ozzy had taught them, but nothing happened. Ozzy fought back the tears as the hope inside begin to fade. Then an idea popped into his head.

"Stand back," he said to the children as he took his blade to the glass wall.

"If this dagger can cut through diamond, then…" Ozzy pressed the blade against the glass. The moment the tip of the blade touched it, thin cracks began to appear, running in different directions from the point. As Ozzy tapped the centre of the fissures, a small opening appeared, just big enough for Ozzy to stare at the commotion outside.

Outside the tower, the drumming grew louder as the silhouettes of the shadow beasts and creatures began to dance and make hideous noises. There was a thunderous crack, as if the very sky was breaking. The vile creatures and shadows lay prostrate on the ground and the drumming silenced. A tall, hooded figure rode through the circle of beasts. He was enveloped in a long black cloak and was astride the body of a purple horse with a bull's head and a snake's tail.

"The Shadow Prince," Ozzy whispered to the children. "Keep very quiet."

The Shadow Prince raised white arms that were coiled in black snakes. He took off his hood and revealed his ugly, terrifying face. His hairless head was metallic rather than fleshly, like the skin of a snake. His eyes were like black holes and flashes of violet light, like electricity, shot through the sockets towards the shadow creatures and beasts. They convulsed as if they had been struck by lightning. When he opened his cavernous mouth, a long and inky forked tongue protruded from it, rattling viciously. Black bats and dark shadows flew above the lava lake, screaming as if they were in terrible pain. Then the Shadow Prince turned to the tower. A horde of shadow monkeys chattered all around him as he laughed and laughed.

"Light is more powerful than darkness!" Ozzy bellowed.

The dark Prince turned his beast towards the tower.

Ozzy turned to the children hiding behind him. "Get back!" he whispered as the Prince and his ghoulish entourage headed towards him.

Just then, Ozzy saw Benji and Flo, their weapons raised, running towards the tower, ready to stand between the children and the Shadow Prince. As the creatures of the night saw them, they shrieked and screamed, trying to terrorise them. As Ozzy looked on, he thrust his dagger into the glass again, this time so hard the surface shattered, like breaking ice on a thawing lake. As the monkeys clambered all over his friends, Ozzy took a step outside into the heat of the battle.

"Stay here!" he shouted to the children, before running to his friends.

"Ozzy!" Flo cried.

The three children formed a triangle, covering every angle, and hurled the monkeys to the ground. The monkeys, enraged, blew darts through their horns but the missiles just bounced off their glowing bodies.

Black snakes slithered across the ground and tried to entangle their legs, but they speared them and then cut off their heads. Whatever the dark creature that tried to attack them, the power they possessed in unity emitted from their bodies like moonbeams. It was so great that the attackers had no answer to it.

All the while, however, the Shadow Prince continued to laugh as though the children's feats were mere entertainment. Then he stopped, lifted his arms towards the black tower and hurled two balls of fire from his hands. The tower shattered into a million fragments.

"No!" Ozzy screamed.

The Shadow Prince walked to the remains of the building. The children were nowhere to be seen.

"Where are they?" the Shadow Prince roared. "Find them!"

The dark shadows scattered.

Ozzy, Benji and Flo ran towards the rubble.

"They've escaped!" Ozzy said. "They were right here. I was with them, looking after them."

"We know," Flo said. "We saw you."

Just then, the Shadow Prince raised his hands and used his power to lift the three friends into the air. They were helpless as electric currents coursed through their bodies.

"Stop!"

The voice was that of a child.

"Joanna!" Benji cried.

She was standing with Bea and Jo, with scores of children were behind her, cowering in her shadow.

The Shadow Prince laughed and dropped the three friends. He looked at Ozzy. "If you want these children to be spared," he roared, "you must choose one of them to be sacrificed today."

"Never!" said Benji, stepping towards the Shadow Prince.

The Shadow Prince laughed, and the earth shook. Hot geysers shot up from the ground and Benji leapt out of the way.

"One child will be sacrificed, and I will let the others go!"

"No!" Ozzy shouted. "You will not harm any child! The Fire King will not allow it!"

The Shadow Prince pointed to little Jo and lifted him into the air, suspending him over the lake of lava. "This one will do!"

"No!" Benji cried.

Just as the Shadow Prince was about to drop the child, Ozzy walked forward and dropped to his knees before the Shadow Prince. "You can have me!" he said.

"What's this?"

"You can have me instead. Just let him go."

Flo gasped.

"I said, let him go!"

"No, Ozzy!" all the children cried.

"Very well," the Shadow Prince said, realising from the response of his friends that Ozzy was the greater prize. "So, then, the little orphan boy wants to be a hero!"

"I'm not an orphan! I'm a Fire Child!" Ozzy shouted. Somehow, he was not afraid anymore. He felt as if the fire within him was greater than the bubbling lava in front of his very eyes.

"No!" Benji and Flo cried.

"It has to be this way," Ozzy shouted. "I have no family."

"But we are your family," Flo cried.

"I know, and coming here with you has been the best time of my life!"

"Enough talk!" the Shadow Prince barked.

In one swift movement, he raised Ozzy high above the mouth of the volcano, just beneath a band of harpies. One swooped down and took Ozzy in the grip of her black claws. As the drums beat wildly, she held him as an offering before the Shadow Prince.

The sky turned pitch black.

The only light came from the glow of the fire.

The dark shadows began to chant and dance in a circle around the ring of fire as the Shadow Prince's face contorted. He made hideous sounds and became even more grotesque as he absorbed their terrible worship.

The harpy dropped Ozzy from a great height into the burning lake.

All the children screamed as his body fell.

Benji and Flo threw themselves to the ground, crying out in defeat.

"Ozzy!" Benji shouted.

"Where is the Fire King?" Flo sobbed.

27
TWO KEYS

As soon as Ozzy hit the scorching lava, he was transported unharmed into the centre of a fire tunnel. He hurtled at great speed down its centre until he landed on the hard, cold ground. He felt his body. No broken bones. No burns. And no smell of smoke. He seemed to be alive, and yet he was standing in a wide-open space of nothingness that seemed to go on forever and ever. It was grey, dark and lifeless.

Just then, Ozzy noticed the voices. They were everywhere, crying and wailing. But he could see no one.

"Where am I?" he cried as he walked in circles. "Where am I?" he repeated.

No response.

Ozzy began to feel consumed with a dreadful feeling of loneliness. All the horrible feelings he had felt on earth, feelings of being alone and rejected, surfaced again, only this time a million times worse. He fell on his knees and cried out, but all he could hear, amongst the wailing, was the sound of his own cries.

Just when he thought he was doomed, a bright light appeared. As it drew nearer, a figure became to form – a great and mighty angel with a face burning as radiantly as a star. The creature had six wings, and his legs and arms were like pillars of fire. Ozzy bowed low before him.

"I am Seraph," the angel said. "Don't be afraid. This is Asunder, the underworld of bodiless souls. You do not belong here."

"Am I dead?" Ozzy asked.

"You will not die. You are immortal."

"Why am I here?"

"The Shadow Prince sent you here, but you don't belong here, and I have permission to give you these."

Seraph gave Ozzy two keys, one gold, the other silver.

"These will open doors inside the Sapphire Palace."

Ozzy took the keys and wiped his eyes. Then Seraph took his hand and they flew high above the bleak wasteland of bodiless souls and far away from the terrible underworld. They rocketed above the black clouds, where the sun shone so brightly that Ozzy had to close his eyes.

28

THE CHAIR

Flo held onto Joanna and Bea and sobbed so much that her head ached. She closed her eyes and started to whisper the battle song. Then all the children began to join in and before long, the sky above them was filled with fire.

"Look!" Flo cried. The children gazed above to see countless angels, all singing the battle song.

As the children continued to sing, the Shadow Prince and all his creatures disappeared like dust. Thousands of luminous butterflies danced above the children as the Moon Queen appeared in front of them. Her iridescent wings seemed to spread across the sky and her long amber hair shone like the sun. She smiled at the children as they ran to her and huddled inside her wings.

"We lost!" Benji cried. "The Shadow Prince has killed Ozzy."

"Ozzy gave his life to save you."

"But he was my friend." The tears were falling now.

"This can't be the end," Flo cried, her fists curled into tight balls.

The Moon Queen displayed her wide wings once again. A white light poured from her body, causing the children to cover their eyes. When they dared to look again, the Moon Queen had gone. They were all stood safely at the shore of Jade Lake, along with a band of fireflies that seemed to radiate as the sun set.

Blaze played his usual tunes and led them all through the woods. The elves and fairies of Lazuli village uttered a loud cheer when they caught sight of the battle-weary children covered in volcanic dust from head to toe.

A friendly elf wheeled a chair over to Joanna. This was no ordinary chair. It was fashioned from silver and rose gold. Angel's wings were engraved on each armrest and tiny blue sapphires and red rubies were embedded in the golden wheels. Joanna sat down on its blue velvet seat and smiled.

"It suits you, Queen Joanna," Benji said as he bowed towards her.

Joanna blushed.

The children laughed but Flo kept quiet.

Up in the tree houses, an enticing aroma of healing oils floated from steamy wooden baths filled with bubbling tree milk and rainbow rose petals. The children took off their tattered clothes and climbed into the soothing liquid. Fireflies brought them fire berry tea and moon muffins.

Later, Flo watched Joanna spin around with the little children, but deep in her heart it just didn't feel right to celebrate without Ozzy. The busyness of it all made her dizzy as she sat with her fists over her ears to drown out the noise. Benji, meanwhile, sat with his face buried in his hands and cried. Seeing this, Flash and Flick made a fire and gave them a calming mug of tea and within seconds, they both fell asleep. Not long afterwards, all the children joined them. Soon, a deep sleep enveloped them all.

29

TWO DOORS

Ozzy reached the top of the steps to the Sapphire Palace, the same palace he had seen before in his dream. Made of solid blue sapphire, it was so high and wide he couldn't see the end of it. Seraph stood at the entrance, his face shining like a bright star. There appeared to be a tall and shimmering glass door next to him. As Ozzy looked closer, he realised it was a waterfall, pounding down before him. He felt a little nervous, but Seraph nodded for him to go, so he took a little step forward, then another, until water drenched him. It fell on his head so hard his body bent underneath the heavy flow. It wasn't an unpleasant sensation. Quite the opposite. The more the water cascaded on top of his head, the more he began to laugh. In fact, he laughed so heartily he couldn't stop. Then the water began to recede, and he found himself standing in a cool breeze blowing on a clear glass floor inside the circular hall of the palace.

The floor under his feet was like a blue, glass sea. The walls looked as if they were made of marble and were illuminated by gold framed pictures of Fire Children over the ages. Each one celebrated the victories they had won.

A wide fireplace made of lapis lazuli contained a great fire. This was no ordinary fire; its flames were of many colours. A low table made of solid oak bore two gold cups in front of the hearth. Two blue velvet chairs were placed by the table. Ozzy's name was written on a gold plaque and on the other was written, The Fire King.

Ozzy sat down.

Then, out of nowhere, the Fire King appeared.

He was tall and strong, and his very presence seemed to charge the room with a powerful energy. His skin was dark, like Ozzy's, and his hair was thick and black. He had a long beard and his eyes emitted a piercing blue fire. They were so full of kindness that Ozzy felt as if he could stare into them forever. He was lost for words.

The Fire King smiled. "Thank you, Ozzy, for the bravery you have shown today. You have defeated the Shadow Prince."

"How? Is he dead?"

"Not yet. That day will come. But because you have performed a great act of love, you will help bring colour back to the earth again."

A warm light permeated the room as angels of fire lined the circular walls. A lion with a fiery mane stood next to each of the angels.

The King looked at Ozzy and, somehow, Ozzy knew in the deepest part of his soul that what he had done that day had been right and good.

"I have one last task for you," the Fire King said. "This requires you to make a very important choice. I have given you two keys and you must decide which door you will go through."

The King pointed to two doors. The door to the left was made of solid gold and the door to the right of oak wood.

"The door to the left will allow you to live here with me always in Everland. What you have seen of Everland so far is just the outskirts. Beyond the palace, there is so much more for you to experience. In this great and glorious landscape, you will never feel any hurt or rejection again."

The King's eyes filled with tears. A tender smile spread across his face. "This is your home," he said. His words were like a rumbling fire. Each angel and each lion knelt and bowed.

"If you choose to go through the door to the left, you must leave earth behind you and never return. However, the door to the right will lead you back to earth. You will be able to take the children home. But it will not be easy. The colour will not quickly return. Most people have lost their hope because the world has plummeted into the deepest darkness it has ever known. The Shadow Prince has taken centre stage."

At the mention of the Shadow Prince, the lions growled while the faces of the angels burned with a raging fire.

"But if you go back and take my children with you, people will see the colour and the Shadow Prince will be defied. When the earth fills with colour again, his power will weaken."

The King picked up his goblet. Ozzy did the same and drank a sip of bright water. At once, his mind became sharp and clear.

"The choice is yours."

Just as quickly as the Fire King had appeared, he vanished, leaving his empty throne behind him.

Ozzy stood and walked to the door that led into Everland. He rested his head and his hands on the golden panelling. He was angry and sad as he thumped the metal.

"Why do I have to choose? Why doesn't the Fire King just kill the Shadow Prince straight away?"

Ozzy didn't like the thought of returning to earth at all. He would have happily stayed in Everland forever. Wasn't it enough that he had just hurled himself into a lake of fire? He didn't have anything on earth to look forward to; everything he could remember was miserable and grey.

But then he thought about Benji and Flo. He really wanted to go wherever they planned to go. He remembered what the Moon Queen told him in his dream. "Ozzy, the Fire King has given you and all the Fire Children a part to play in bringing the colour back. Will you help him?"

Ozzy shook his head and tried to ignore her words. "I don't want to go back," he cried, but he knew what he had to do.

Ozzy stepped towards the wooden door to the right, holding the silver key in his hand. The door handle was made of iron. It was in the shape of a sun and it had the Fire King's head festooned upon it.

Ozzy turned the silver key and the door swung open. A cold wind engulfed him. He took hold of a lantern by the door and it burst into a bright, blue flame.

Ozzy crossed the threshold into the dark thick forest of Witch Woods.

Everland now lay behind him.

30

ROBIN

Mrs Brook stood at her kitchen window, washing the dishes over and over again. They were spotless ten minutes ago, but when she was anxious, she would clean things repeatedly until her hands were sore. She stared at herself in the reflection of the glass. She looked like a ghost; her complexion was as white as the sky through the window. She arched her brows and took short, sharp breaths as she thought about her missing boys.

How had they just vanished?

It had been two days and she hadn't eaten a crumb of food and was feeling faint. She closed her eyes and began to hum an old tune her dad used to sing to her as a little girl. Little did she know she was repeating the melody to the battle song.

"The boys will bring the colour back. You just wait and see."

He had said these words as he breathed his last breath.

Just as she remembered, she opened her eyes and looked out of her kitchen window to see a tiny robin perched on the colourless tree. At once, her heart fluttered as she noticed the robin's breast was no longer grey but a lovely red again. It tilted towards her, bowing its head, and then off it flew into the pallid sky. She took a long, deep breath and a flame of hope flickered inside her.

Meanwhile, Mr Brook sat on the white leather barstool, sipping his black coffee with his dark eyes fixed on the enormous TV on their dining room wall. He hadn't slept for days. A grave sounding newsman was reporting the missing children all around the world. Mr Brook's sons' faces appeared on the huge TV, along with thirteen other children. His eyes swelled with tears.

As the sky was darkening, the phone rang.

Mrs Brook sprang from the kitchen counter.

"Hello. Yes, this is Mr Brook… Oh thank God! Yes, yes! We are on our way!"

He looked at his wife. "Some children have been found in Witch Woods! Let's go!"

Mrs Brook's eyes widened. Her hands fell to her sides. And the glass vase she was buffing smashed into a thousand pieces on the ground.

31

ALIVE

A bright, white light shone into Benji's eyes as he stirred from his deep slumber on a bed of leaves. A tall grey, gangly figure carrying a torch was moving towards him. Flo and all the other children were still sleeping like kittens in front a waning campfire in the middle of Witch Woods.

A large lady with big hair shuffled forward. "We've found them!" she shouted as she picked up a big stick and prodded the children. "And they're alive!"

Mr Crouch and Mrs Electra shouted hysterically and blew their whistles, just as five policemen came bounding up Witch Wood path with their sniffer dogs. Flo covered her ears and all the children sat up.

"Where have the fairies and the fireflies gone?" Jo cried.

"What happened, how did we get here?" Flo asked, looking disoriented.

"Children!" Mr Crouch's torchlight fixed upon them.

"Good grief children, where on earth have you been?" Mrs Electra cried.

The policemen shone their torches into each child's face.

"What is going on here?" a policeman asked. He was confused to discover that their faces were full of colour.

"Stand back! Stand back!" another shouted. "There's something strange going on here. It may not be safe."

The third policeman spoke into his radio. "Children found alive! I repeat, children found! They have colour. I repeat, they have colour! I can see blonde hair, brown hair, brown eyes and blue."

The fourth police officer counted the children. "And there are in fact fifteen children here, not five. Fifteen, I repeat fifteen!" she cried.

"They are no threat," the fifth shouted. "They are the lost children, for goodness sake." She wrapped blankets around them and offered each one some water to drink.

"Fire berry tea, please." The words came from a little boy with big brown eyes and brown skin.

"I'm afraid I don't have any… And in any case, what on earth is it?" It was the first police officer's voice.

"How long have we been gone?" Benji asked, jumping to his feet and spinning around.

"Two full days!" Mr Crouch said. He was looking older and greyer than ever.

"What day is it?" Benji asked. "What time is it?"

Just then, a troop of police on motorbikes appeared, along with an ambulance, their blue lights rotating in the darkness. Benji was even more excited now; he had always wanted to be part of a police investigation.

"It's Sunday and it's 9pm!" Mr Crouch answered as a flurry of frenzied parents came running down Witch Wood path towards their children. Star bounded in front of them and leapt into Flo's arms.

"Oh Star, I've missed you!" she said.

As Flo cuddled him, something extraordinary happened. The animal's peppery grey fur changed into amber gold – the same colour she had when she was a puppy, before the world turned grey.

"Do you see that, Flo?" Benji asked.

Mrs Brook ran towards Benji and Jo. "Where have you two been?" she screamed. She was angry for a moment, and then she broke into deep sobs and squeezed them tightly. "I thought you were dead. I have been worried sick!" Then she gazed at them. "Your eyes, my darlings. They're blue! And your hair is blonde again! How can this be?"

Benji couldn't tell if she was happy or sad. She hugged him so hard he thought he might pop.

"Mum!" Jo shouted. "We were taken by the flying witches to a big volcano. The Shadow Prince wanted to kill us, but Ozzy saved us. He's a hero!"

"Ozzy?" Benji asked.

"What on earth are you talking about?" Mr Brook interjected. "What stories have you been filling their heads with, Benji?"

"Don't tell him off, Steve," Mrs Brook said. "Listen to them!" The colour in her eyes had already begun to return.

Then out of the deep, dark thick of the woods, a small blue light shone in the distance.

"What's that?" Benji asked, leaping to his feet. "Flo, look!"

Flo stood up and the blanket around her shoulders fell to the ground. "Is it Cast?" she asked as her eyes lit up.

The small blue light grew bigger.

"It's Ozzy!" Benji shouted.

"You're alive!" Flo cried.

Ozzy weaved between the trees and waded through the thick overgrowth, all the while holding onto his glass lantern.

Benji followed Flo, who ran into Ozzy so hard that they all fell laughing into a heap.

"You don't look wounded," Flo said after they had calmed down.

"Did it burn?" Benji asked.

"What?"

"The fire, the volcano! How are you not dead?"

"I fell into Asunder." Ozzy was shivering.

"Where's that?"

"A place far more horrid than earth, and I didn't think that was possible. It's hard to explain. It was empty and awful. I could hear lots of crying and screaming but I couldn't see where it was coming from. It was like there were voices, but no bodies. Then Seraph appeared and gave me two keys, and then…"

"Ozzy Stone!" Mr Crouch interrupted. "I was wondering where you were hiding. You had better come with me!" The teacher tried to reach the children, but he became tangled up in the undergrowth.

Just then, Ozzy's uncle appeared. He yanked Ozzy's elbow. His face seemed contorted and worn.

"We haven't quite got to the bottom of this, Mr Stone," Mr Crouch said, bending his head towards him like a giraffe. "But we will be calling in the parents and carers of the children that went missing to give a full statement when we do."

Even though Mr Crouch was a clear foot taller than Mr Stone, he still trembled in his presence. Mr Stone just ignored him. He clearly had no time for teachers or the police. He walked off, dragging Ozzy with him. "No games console for you when you get home," he said in a deep and gravely tone.

Ozzy looked down and sighed. He couldn't care less about the games console anymore, but he was beginning to wish he had chosen to go through the door to Everland.

No sooner had they left than the crowd of children and parents hobbled back up the icy path towards the school building.

Mr Crouch raised his voice. "All we can do, ladies and gentlemen, is once again apologise for the last two days. Thankfully, your children are safe and unharmed. I will be working closely with the police and

I will be in touch with you all on Monday morning. We'll find out what really happened. And we'll find the culprit!" Mr Crouch stared at Ozzy as he was being led away.

Some of the children shook their heads.

"It's not Ozzy's fault!" Benji shouted. He waved to Ozzy and Ozzy turned around and grinned. It was in that moment his hope returned. He knew he'd made the right decision to come back, because for the first time in his life, he had two best friends and there was no way he was going to let them go.

32

BIG PRUNERS

Back home, Mrs Brook called from the hallway. "Benji! Jo! Get your coats on! We're going to see your grandma!"

Benji punched the air and slid down the bannister. Little Jo copied him.

"I've never seen you this cheery to visit your grandma before," she said. "And how many times have I told you not to slide down the bannister?"

As they stepped outside, they were greeted by a crowd of news reporters between the doorstep and the car. Benji looked at them. He grinned and then ran towards the holly tree at the bottom of the garden. He did a somersault. Right before the reporters' beady eyes, the grass turned bright green, as did the dull grey leaves on the evergreen tree. Their little berries burst into red.

The journalists gasped and snapped away with their cameras as Mrs Brook shouted, "Benji, get into the car at once!"

"Mrs Brook, would you be kind enough to allow your sons to answer some very important questions?" The request came from a rather persistent news reporter with thick round glasses and a recording device in his hand.

"I'm sorry! We must go."

Mrs Brook climbed into the car.

The reporters shuffled over to the evergreen tree, taking pictures and marvelling at the colour as Mrs Brook drove away.

"Look at that stretch of sky!" she said, pointing above Brook Cottage. It was blue and cloudless. Although the day was cold, the bright sun took the edge off it as they all clambered out of the car.

"Who is that?" Mrs Brook cried as they approached the garden. "Is it your grandma? She hasn't been out in the garden for years!"

Mrs Brook rushed to the garden gate to see her mum standing next to the enormous television that had once been fixed to the chimney breast. It had been dumped in the middle of the garden.

"Mum! What's going on?"

Grandma Brook stood in front of her red ivy-covered cottage, raking copper leaves in her denim blue dungarees, and a large straw sombrero. The garden was bursting with browns, copper and yellow colours. Purple and white crocuses grew wild across the unkempt lawn, lined with evergreen and red maple trees.

As she heard them, she turned with one arm waving and the other holding the rake. "Hello!" she called. She had a big smile and her little blue eyes twinkled above her rosy cheeks. "I'm just doing a spot of gardening. Isn't it a stunning day?" Then she looked at her daughter. "Now Harriet, do you know where I put my big pruners? I can't find them in the shed. It's a terrible mess in there!"

"Mum, what on earth is going on? Shouldn't you be inside? How's your head? Is that the TV?"

"Ah, I have no use for that silly thing, taking up far too much space. My headaches are gone, my dear!"

Grandma Brook winked and Benji and Jo giggled.

"And aren't you the one who is always telling me I need some fresh air?" she asked with a chuckle. "I feel twenty years younger since

Benji gave me that rainbow leaf!"

"What? When?"

"Oh yeah, I forgot to tell you!" Benji said.

"Tell me what?"

"About a dream that turned out not to be a dream!"

Mrs Brook looked confused.

"Your dad was right, Harriet," Grandma Brook said. "All his talk of fighting the shadows with the Fire King, it's all true, my dear. I just never wanted to believe it, but then I ate the leaf and I saw the most beautiful light fill my living room. Oh Harriet, after all these years, I know your dad was right!"

"I need a cup of tea," Mrs Brook replied, looking a little faint.

33

RAINBOW

Flo stirred in her patchwork bed. The patches were no longer grey and white but poppy red, deep purple, mustard and teal. She had been dreaming of making fire berry jam in the Elfin Glades when she opened her eyes to see that she was at home and little Bea was safe in the bed beside her. She smiled with relief as she looked up to see all her black-and-white sketches of animals and mini beasts turn to colour, but there was a deep longing in her heart for more adventures. She looked outside her window as the white sun rose in a cold November sky.

Flo began to hum the battle song and Bea woke up and joined her. The girls giggled and started to play. Flo took the white sheet from her bed and placed it around her shoulders, pretending to be the Moon Queen. The girls laughed as everything they touched turned to colour.

The next moment, Mrs Knightly came into the room. "I can see you are both feeling fine this morning. Let's have some breakfast and a little chat."

Minutes later, the girls were staring into their bowls of porridge as their mum and dad waited to hear what they had to say.

"We have been so worried about you girls." Mrs Knightly was on the edge of tears. "Where on earth were you? Who took you? Was it that Ozzy Stone?"

"Let's hear what the girls have to say," Mr Knightly said.

Flo looked deep into her mum's eyes. "Don't blame Ozzy. We were taken into another realm. It's right here, but it's invisible. We had to fight many battles, but we won! Bea, Jo and Joanna and all the stolen children were taken to the top of Black Mountains and we had to save them!"

"So, you were playing a game," Mr Knightly said.

"We were locked inside a big black tower. Ozzy saved us and then the Moon Queen came, and we went back to Lazuli and saw fireflies and fairies!" Bea added.

Mr Knightly smiled. "It sounds very exciting, Bea. Is this the game you were playing in the woods?"

"No Daddy, this was at the top of a mountain!"

Jen sighed and turned to Flo. "Flo, you are old enough and intelligent enough to be sensible. Tell us the truth about what happened."

"Bea is telling you the truth, Mum. I know it sounds unbelievable, but it's all true."

Mr Knightly looked angry. "I think we need to call the child psychologist. This has gone too far."

Mrs Knightly burst into tears and left the kitchen.

Flo's heart sank like a stone as she looked at her dad. He was very cross. Flo began to cry too as she tightened her fists into tight balls.

"Don't worry, Flo, the Fire King will help us," Bea said.

Flo wiped away her tears and looked out of the window. The sky was white but as she looked at it and thought about the Fire King, it began to turn a light shade of blue.

"Yes, Bea. He will." Flo wiped her tears away. The courage she had felt when she first took hold of the sword of stones began to rise within her heart. "He will."

Mr Knightly shook his head.

"You girls are grounded for two weeks. I don't know what has got into your heads. That Ozzy Stone seems no good, and I do wonder about Benji Brook. His grandpa was always a bit strange."

"Jo was a lovely man, Tom," Mrs Knightly said. She had just returned to the kitchen. "He would do anything for anyone, and Benji is a lovely boy. We can't take Flo's best friend away. It's most likely something to do with Ozzy Stone. There's no other explanation."

"Well, I don't think the girls should be around Benji either, for a while at least. They should be at home doing their maths homework. They spend too much time playing outside and climbing trees anyway."

"They are children!" she said. "Children need to play and be outdoors! Don't be so uptight, Tom!"

"Uptight? Perhaps I've got that from you!"

Flo was now enraged. "What's wrong with both of you?" she exploded, her face a fiery red and her eyes bulging. "Life isn't just what you see here in this black-and-white world. And, in any case, can't you see that it's filling with colour again?"

Flo's parents didn't know what to say. They couldn't deny that her colour had returned, and she was braver than they ever thought possible. Something very strange was going on.

"Calm down, Flo. It's okay. Can you and Bea go to your room, so we can talk?" Her mum spoke gently, holding onto Flo's tight fists with both hands.

"No!" Flo screamed as she pulled away and groaned. "Why can't I tell you all about the penguins and how they like to swim and not fly, and about the fireflies too?" She ran to her room and slammed the door.

"The fireflies are real!" Bea yelled as she stamped on the ground and ran after Flo, joining her in her room.

While Flo sobbed into her pillow, Bea began to sing.

Arise!

Arise!

Arise!

Flo sat up and started to sing through her tears.

As they sang, downstairs Mr Knightly was standing on the furry rug, looking like he had been punched in the stomach. Flo's words were echoing in his mind as he stared out of the window and up at the dark clouds filling the sky.

Just then, a little light appeared at the window.

Rainbow the butterfly fluttered into the room, glowing like a moonbeam.

He stared at the creature. Then he looked at his wife and his hard heart began to crack. He hadn't cried for years. He had felt so sad about the death of his daughter, but he had never allowed himself to cry. Yet, in that moment, he couldn't help himself, as the tears began to gush from his eyes. Jen looked up with surprise etched on her face as her husband released an avalanche of pain.

They looked at each other and hugged.

Then they watched the butterfly dance across the living room.

As it flew past their teary faces, a burst of colours appeared.

Then it flew through the window into the cold, blue November sky.

34

CHRISTMAS

It was Christmas Eve and the grand old hall of Kingswick flickered like a gigantic birthday cake. Thousands of fairy lights flashed around every window and along the wide roof under the twilight sky.

A brass band stood at the foot of a stone staircase leading to a tall doorway into a circular hall hosting a great open fire. On the walls were old oil paintings of dragons, beasts and warriors fighting among angelic and dark creatures under a full moon.

A twelve-foot Christmas tree dressed in warm lights sat beside the musicians as the choir prepared to sing. Families were wrapped snugly in black-and-white hats, scarves and gloves. Yet, dotted across the crowd was a splash of red and bottle green, burnt orange, purple and gold as the people of Kingswick warmed themselves with mulled wine, hot blackcurrant and fresh mince pies.

Benji's classmates waved their phones in the air and pointed to him. He was wearing his red, chunky, bobble hat. A group of girls giggled and blushed as he stopped to have a quick selfie with them. Holding his mandolin in one hand, he high fived them with the other. Benji was no longer the class nuisance; he was something of a celebrity as he weaved his way through the crowd, waving at the cameras on his way to Flo, Ozzy and Joanna, who were also dressed in warm, bright colours. The children ducked and dived to the bottom of the icy stone steps of the old hall, where two stone lions sat either side.

Mrs Brook stood behind a table of steaming mugs of hot chocolate, toasting marshmallows in a firepit. Benji chose the mug with the biggest mountain of whipped cream. Drooling, he sank his teeth into a melting marshmallow squished between two digestive biscuits.

Weeks had passed since the eve of Halloween and the adventures into Battlelands. Although the children could no longer find the spiralling steps inside the hollow tree, or sing their way into another land, their colour remained and spread wherever they went.

It was the talk of Kingswick and beyond.

In fact, it was all over the news. Although Flo was getting fed up of reporters sticking cameras in her face and asking questions, Benji quite liked it. It turned out that there were sightings of colourful children appearing in every country, all over the world.

The children lit up like moonbeams every time they thought about the Fire King. Some people would stop and stare and wonder at them, marvelling at the colours, but some shook their heads and thought it was a trick. Others were so lost in their own misery that they didn't even believe what was right in front of their eyes.

Ozzy was a changed boy. His eyes were bright and kind, and if you looked closely enough, they would flicker like small flames. He was a magnet for the younger children. He wore a golden key on a leather string around his neck and whenever they asked him why he had it, he would simply say, "It's my key back to Everland."

Mr Stone stood beside Ozzy and patted him on the shoulder. The people of Kingswick would look aghast at Mr Stone smiling for the first time in fifty years. He had pearl white teeth, like piano keys, and although his change from grey to brown was very slow, his skin soon took on a beautiful mahogany colour. There was a flush of pink in his old shrivelled cheeks and his eyes shone like tiger stones. It turned out that he grew quite fond of his nephew; the people of Kingswick would see them by the lake, every Sunday afternoon, skimming stones together.

Since the day Mr Knightly burst into tears, he couldn't stop crying. Not in a bad way. After every tear fell, his heart would feel lighter and a joy would bubble up and make him giggle. Then everyone else would giggle too.

Mrs Knightly couldn't deny that the change in her husband's heart was miraculous, nor that Flo had become so very brave. She began to believe that perhaps there was a little bit of truth in the fantastical tales. It wasn't long before the whole household was filled with brilliant colours again.

The Knightlys even threw a special party to renew their wedding vows and announce to their close friends that they were going to have another baby. Bea and Joanna wore their moon boots, under long white dresses, and they looked like mini Moon Queens. Flo wore her rainbow leggings and silver top and played their battle song on the piano. Benji, Jo and Ozzy played adventure games with their weapons. It was quite remarkable that none of the adults had twigged that the bejewelled weapons were real, even when Benji spun his spear in the air and its golden tip would burst into flame.

The adults celebrated with sparkly wine and moon muffins that Grandma Brook had baked. They weren't as good as the oozing and mind-bogglingly delicious moon muffins the children had eaten in Battlelands, but they were close enough.

As Benji, Flo and Ozzy stood at the foot of the stone stairs in front of the old hall, the sky resembled a lilac canopy. Their eyes lit up as soft flecks of snow fell from the sky and Rainbow lit up like a moonbeam.

The hairs on their skin stood on end as they heard their song in the sky.

Arise!

Arise!

Arise!

Benji began to play his mandolin and then out of nowhere, as the brass band and the people of Kingswick began to join in with their voices and instruments, the sky filled with fire. Every adult and child stood in awe as the sky throbbed with the fiery light of a thousand angels. One reporter scribbled notes and clicked away with his camera as the people of Kingswick scrambled about, whipping out their phones to snap away, but the fire in the sky faded before they had a chance to capture it.

The children looked across the clearing and saw their favourite oak tree in the light of the setting sun. A tall, dark hooded figure stood beside it and a few shadows seemed to scatter and shift and then vanish into thin air, but this didn't seem to bother them at all.

Benji looked down to see something glow and move inside Flo's pocket. She put her hand inside and her eyes widened with surprise as she pulled her closed fist out to see it was glowing. It was Blaze the firefly, winking in the palm her hand.

The children stood together under the crimson clouds. They looked up to see the bright eyes of their Fire King in the sky, and it was at that very moment they knew he would always be with them. Although to some witnesses, this looked just like a sunset, they knew, deep in their hearts, that it was so much more than that.

The children had seen the miracle of colour return and a fire begin to burn in their eyes. They had seen for themselves that the light will always be stronger than the darkness. And even though in some ways their battles had only just begun, they would never give up believing what Grandpa Brook had said.

Colour will return to those who believe...

Sure enough, Benjamin Brook, Florence Knightly and Ozzy Stone knew from that day on that they were never meant to blend into the grey spaces. They were always meant to stand out and be a splash of colour on the black-and-white canvas of this world.

Acknowledgements

I would first like to thank my husband Theo for his love and sacrifice. You give me the space to dream and create. Thank you for supporting me, cheering me on and believing in me when I didn't believe in myself.

Thank you Noah and Joseph, our bold and brilliant sons. Let us always go on wild adventures to explore the beauty and wonders of the seen and the unseen. You are my greatest inspiration. I wrote this story for you, for your fire children, for their fire children and all the fire children!

And a heart-felt thank you to Matilda, Ramona and Seth Porter for joining us on our many adventures. Watching you all explore nature and play freely in the forests and the wide-open-spaces has helped paint the words across these pages.

Thank you, Mum and Dad for being my biggest fans. Thank you, Mum, for loving everything I do, even if I think it's a flop you manage to see the beauty in it. And thank you Dad, my great advisor and zealous encourager, thanks for loving my crazy imagination and basking in the brilliant thought that where we are is merely a shadow of where we really belong.

Thank you, Jan and Ian Bebbington, for your insurmountable support, daily prayers over this project and my life in general. I would not be where I am today if it weren't for your faithfulness. There's a truckload of treasure in heaven for you guys!

And thank you to Dr Mark Stibbe who has been my tremendous writing coach and editor. Writing this book has been a challenging and humbling experience. It has been a privilege to learn from you and having you be the first to edit my debut story was a bit like someone coming along and sprinkling it with a pinch of gold dust.

Above all, thanks to my readers, for daring to believe that there is more to life than meets the eye. That beyond the grey spaces there are many colours, more colours than we thought possible. Look out for those small white butterflies that flutter freely, and if you look closely enough you might just see their rainbow trails.